Tony Saint was born in Northumberland in 1968 and educated at the taxpayers' expense. After attending university in Bristol and Hamilton, Ontario, he joined the United Kingdom Immigration Service in 1993. He lives with his wife in South London. *Refusal Shoes* is his first novel.

refusal shoes

Tony Saint

Library of Congress Catalog Card Number: 2003101111

A complete catalogue record for this book can be obtained from the British Library on request

The characters and events in this book are fictitious. Any similarity to real persons, living or dead, is coincidental and not intended by the author.

First published in 2003 by Serpent's Tail,
4 Blackstock Mews, London N4 2BT

website: www.serpentstail.com

Printed by Mackays of Chatham plc

10 9 8 7 6 5 4 3 2

contents

To Mum and Dad

prologue

Peter Onions (pronounced O'Nines) took three paracetamol, washing them down with the lukewarm remains of his cup of tea. He'd never taken more than two paracetamol before, but didn't notice any immediate effect.

He sat, looking down at his kitchen table and the money that lay there, still cold to the touch after half an hour out of the freezer, where he had hidden it in a tea caddy.

Four thousand pounds. In used notes, apparently.

It meant nothing. Not any more. Not after what had happened.

The shame of it!

After everything he worked for, the Open University degree, all those language GCSEs and now, with the divorce finally through and promotion so close . . . to throw it all away . . .

He threw two more paracetamol into his mouth. His tongue flexed at the awful taste. Quickly, he got up, went to the cupboard, grabbed the bottle of Bols Chocolate liqueur that was left over from Christmas and swigged the disintegrating pills down. With uncharacteristic recklessness, he took another large, glutinous draught. He felt sick as a result. The prospect of tasting another paracetamol was unbearable.

He filled the kettle and switched it on.

The shame!

At least he had done the right thing by writing the letter, he thought. He gained some pleasure from the knowledge that the letter would put a stop to Thorough once and for all, that he'd never be able to prey on the weaknesses of another, make somebody else betray the service . . . that bastard. Even now he felt afraid of him.

The kettle started to rumble. He didn't want it to boil, so he turned and took a mug from the cupboard over the sink. It had the words DON'T ASK ME, I ONLY WORK HERE *inscribed around the outside. He had meant to take it into the office as his other cup had developed a stubborn stain on the inside and had become chipped at the rim. Nothing worse than drinking from a chipped cup . . .*

He put two tablespoons of honey into the mug and then poured the rest of the bottle of paracetamol in, maybe thirty or forty tablets, filling it with warm water and stirring several times. Then, seizing it with both hands, he sat once more at the kitchen table and proceeded to drain the entire concoction in one go.

He pushed the money out to the edges of the table and pulled the white envelope containing the letter from his shirt pocket. He lay it down before him and gently rested his head on top.

He died patiently.

Eight hours later, a Chinese man in his thirties, dressed in jeans and a black leather jacket, came in by the back door. He had anticipated having to break and enter, but the door had not been locked.

When he found the man dead, a trail of coffee-coloured gunk issuing from his open mouth, he was surprised; he'd only come to scare him, tie him up, knock him about, make sure he was persuaded that going to the police would be a mistake. Now he'd been saved the trouble.

Which left the question of the money on the table. He felt his mood lighten for the first time in the two weeks he'd been in this rotten country, since the long journey in the back of the lorry, flat on his belly for four days in a tiny gap below the driver's cabin. He felt humiliated by travelling in such circumstances, as he had felt humiliated when they had asked him to fix this middle-aged white man who had threatened to talk, now lying dead on the kitchen table. As if he needed to prove his loyalty. Had he not sworn the thirty-six oaths of loyalty to the clan? Did he not wear the black star tattoo on the back of his hand that only its members were entitled to? That should have been enough. It was as if they trusted the tall man, Thorough, more than they trusted their own.

He took all the money and shoved it in his pockets. Rummaging in the anorak hanging off the back of the chair, he found a wallet containing cash and credit cards and took that as well. There was a diary too. He would take the letter. It would prove that he'd done as he was asked. The money he'd keep for himself. It would help him get a passport and ticket out of here. He had no wish to remain now that he knew Xiao was coming. Ever since he had arrived, all he had heard was Xiao, Xiao, Xiao. What were they thinking about, welcoming such a loose cannon into the circle? Wherever Xiao went, trouble followed . . .

A thought struck him. He seized a pen from the table and taking the diary he had found in the dead man's pocket, wrote the name Xiao Ping *as an entry for Sunday, the day they had let slip he was coming. When the police saw that, they'd be looking out for him. With any luck, that would put paid to the troublemaker once and for all.*

With his tattooed hand, the black star scratched beneath the skin, he grabbed the dead man by the hair and pulled up the head, sliding the letter out and putting the diary in its place, just so they wouldn't miss it.

He let the head drop forward and it struck the table with a heavy thud. The Chinese man wiped his hand on the side of his trousers and looked at the corpse contemptuously.

Immigration Officers, *he thought.* Scum of the earth.

chapter 1

bad business

Sunday – Late Shift

Henry Brinks goes in to work the back way. Not one for the grand entrance, not even after three weeks on leave. Just creep in, keep a low profile.

The back way takes you in the far end of the office, through the clerical room. The clerical staff work only Monday to Friday. Today is Sunday, and Henry expects it to be empty.

It is not.

There are two men standing by the photocopier. Henry recognises one, a fellow Immigration Officer. A colleague. *Colleague?* Even after five years here, the thought makes Henry want to throw up.

The other Immigration Officer's name is Simon Topp. He's big, maybe six inches taller than Henry, ruddy, wearing the same blue chinos and white cotton shirt he always wears, sleeves rolled up, collar open, blue knitted tie tugged askew.

He beckons Henry over.

The other man is small, stooped, dressed in a white shirt and trousers that are too long, scratching stubble below his ear. He is from Bangladesh. A Bangla.

Henry walks to the photocopier.

'Give us a hand,' says Simon quietly. The Bangla is not supposed to be in the office. 'I've been trying to get this toerag to cough for two hours. Reckons this is his.'

Simon waves a small purple booklet. A British passport.

Henry looks down at the man.

'It my pattpot,' says the man.

Simon shakes his head. He points to the photocopier.

'Have you seen one of these before?'

The Bangla shakes his head.

Simon turns to Henry.

'My colleague will tell you what it is.'

Henry looks at the photocopier, then at the man.

'Lie detector,' says Henry with a sigh.

The Bangla blinks.

'That's right,' says Simon. 'This machine can tell us whether or not you're telling the truth. What do you think of that?'

The Bangla shuffles, says nothing.

'Right,' Simon continues. 'I'm going to ask you a question, then you press the button and the machine will say whether it's true or whether you're a lying little scrote.'

The Bangla looks at Henry, who just blinks.

Simon waves the passport again.

'Who does this passport belong to?' he asks.

'It my pattpot.'

'Push the button,' sighs Simon.

The Bangla pushes the green button and steps back as the machine whirs and rattles.

'Look,' says Simon. 'Here comes the answer.'

The Bangla strains his neck to see a sheet of paper emerge from the photocopier. Simon holds it up. There is one word printed upon it. **LIE**.

Panic dances across the Bangla's face.

'Well?' asks Simon with a sniff.

'It is true. Not my pattpot.'

Simon nods. 'Thank fuck for that,' he comments. 'Come on,' he says. 'Let's find out who you really are.'

He leads the Bangla away, whispering in Henry's ear as he passes. 'Get rid of the evidence. Don't want to wind up on the front of Amnesty's newsletter.'

Henry laughs.

'You heard about Onions?' says Simon on his way out.

'No. What?'

'Dead.'

'You're kidding?'

'Dead.'

Henry widens his eyes, wants to know more, but Simon Topp and the Bangla are gone. He lifts up the cover on the photocopier and removes the sheet of paper with LIE written on it in black marker pen. Crumpling it, he throws it in the bin before making his way out and down the long corridor towards the rest of the office.

He stops at the door and shuts his eyes, imagining who's inside, imagining what they see when they look up at him as he enters. *Oh, look who's here, pretentious sod, says he's not staying, been here five years, after your five there's no way out . . .*

Or maybe they look up and just see a twenty-eight-year-old in a zip-up fleece with hunched shoulders and bags under his eyes from half a decade of shiftwork.

Sunday, he tells himself. Double time. Just remember the double time.

He opens the door.

And Xiao sits and waits. Not long now, he tells himself, sitting forward and upright, shoulders rigid, hands on lap, staring out of the window as he has done for almost the entire journey, even when there was nothing to see below but clouds. But the clouds are starting to break now, and he can make out fields and the occasional red rooftop.

He hears one of the stewardesses talking to a passenger nearby. 'We'll be landing shortly,' she says. 'Perhaps now,' she adds, 'would be a good time for anyone who needs to use the lavatory . . .'

He throws a glance in her direction and sees that she is looking straight back at him. As their eyes meet, she nods towards the back of the cabin and he blinks his understanding.

With one simple movement, he is up and pushing past his neighbour, offering no apology.

Once in the aisle of the rumbling 737, he heads to the toilet.

Henry goes in.

The room is large, rectangular. The walls are painted a strange yellow-brown, but the predominant colour is the grey of the rows of iron lockers on one wall and the banks of plastic pigeonholes on another. On the left is a door to a small annexe where forgery examinations are undertaken in near darkness. Straight ahead is the heavy black door which leads out on to the immigration control.

Henry is, as ever, unprepared for the unpitying blast of cold air as he enters the office. Although it is November, the room's twin air-conditioners are blowing hard. Everywhere, cardigans are pulled tight and jacket lapels are turned up in self-defence.

Henry walks towards his locker on the far wall. The large tables which furnish the office, some pushed together to create vast workspaces, are littered with plastic coffee cups, discarded files, photocopies of passport pages and tickets, reams of unwanted paper the computers have churned out after mysterious instructions.

He passes Daniella. She's sitting, reading a magazine, brushing her long black hair away from her face and those warm, chocolate eyes. She and Henry started at Terminal C on the same day. Henry is attracted to her, a little less so now that she is going out with Paul Speerpoint, blue-eyed boy of the office with 300-plus refusals a year. Henry harbours fantasies of stabbing out Speerpoint's eyes with a compass. This has led to a cooling between him and Daniella, at least in his own mind.

'All right?' Henry greets her.

'Haven't seen you for ages,' she says, tugging downwards gently on his fleece as he stands by her.

'I've been on leave.'

'Where'd you go?'

'Didn't go anywhere.'

This is not strictly true. He did go home to see his parents but couldn't bear to stay more than a weekend, driven out by his father's ceaseless enquiries about the possibilities of promotion and reminders of how well his brother, a computer engineer living out in California, was doing.

'I'm no expert,' his mother kept saying, usually while she was cooking and thus able to avoid eye contact, 'but he does seem to be doing very well.'

'And what – I'm a failure?'

'I didn't say that. I would never say that. Nor would your father . . .'

'Mum, can we just change the subject . . .'

And then she looked at him with her upset look.

'Why not change the subject? Everything else about you has changed. Sometimes I wonder if you're on drugs, you're so bloody spaced out all the time . . .'

'Oh, God . . .'

'I like your hair,' says Daniella with a knowing smile.

Henry runs his hand through it, self-consciously. Back from his parents' in a fit of rebellious pique and too chicken to have a tattoo, he'd had his mop dyed peroxide-blond. But that was two weeks ago and he's forgotten about it as his own mousy colour has started to reassert itself at the roots.

'I was, you know, bored,' he explains.

'I like it,' she purrs. 'It makes you look a bit . . . dangerous.'

Absurdly, he feels tongue-tied, unsure how to play her insinuation. He changes the subject. 'I just heard about Onions.'

Daniella's eyes widen. 'Oh, yeah. Killed himself.'

Henry gasps. 'How?'

'Pills.'

'No way. I mean . . . Jesus, I mean . . . why?'

'Of course,' she says, flapping the magazine shut, dropping her voice to a whisper. 'You would have missed it. It happened, like, two weeks ago.'

'What did?'

'He got suspended from work.'

'Fuck me.'

This is more surprising than hearing he's committed suicide. Onions is – was – the quintessential textbook Immigration Officer, spoke eight languages, able to spot a forgery at fifty paces, could expose lies in an instant and yet defused difficult situations with the mastery of a trained negotiator. A bit of an old woman, but always popular with everyone in the office, except for the most sociopathic. Henry suspects that the generosity of Peter's character had a lot to do with being called Onions but even he liked him, found him pleasant in a low-intensity sort of a way.

'Suspended?' he repeats.

Daniella leans forward, distractingly close to Henry, lowering her voice still further, something which Henry finds dangerously arousing.

'Nobody's sure, but the talk is that he was nabbed facilitating.'

Facilitating illegal entry, this means.

Henry looks at her in disbelief. 'Peter?'

She pouts and nods, returning to her reading. Henry carries on through the office, shaking his head.

⋆

Seated at the furthest table is Dave Niblo, back straight, keen as mustard. It's hard to pick up names here, but Henry has known Dave's since his first day at Terminal C, when Dave chose to give Henry the benefit of his wisdom as to how to get on. What Henry knows now was that Dave, at that time, had been there himself for only six months. Dave would fail to see the joke in this, for in truth he had been an IO (Immigration Officer), ready to serve and protect, from the moment sperm and egg fused in his mother's tubes. His enthusiasm could blind you to his fundamental lack of ability, but only for so long.

Niblo sits, in the same polyester shirt and Tin-Tin tie he always wears, bending back hard the spine of a worn green passport, rubbing the pages hard with his thumbnail, holding it up repeatedly to the artificial light.

'This passport's *duff*,' says Dave. 'Duff as old boots. Duff as *fuck*. I'm telling you. Duff as fucking . . . Duff as fucking anything.' He leans forward. 'You see here,' Dave says, pointing something out, 'that embossing. Look at the quality. I reckon that's duff. Well fucking duff. Here, Henry, what'cha reckon?'

He hands the passport to Henry, who gives it a cursory look. Five years in the job and he still doesn't know a forgery from a bull's foot.

'What you reckon?' says Dave. 'Duff as old boots. Embossing's not right. You see, there.'

'No Julius,' comments Henry, tossing the passport disdainfully down on the desk.

Julius. Julius Caesar. Visa.

'Niger,' Dave says, picking it up again and inspecting the nationality emblazoned on the front. 'What do you call someone from Niger? Nigerians come from Nigeria, so who comes from Niger?'

Henry ignores Dave, knowing what he's getting at.

'Fucking duffers, that's who,' says a deep voice from behind him.

Henry turns.

Thorough. It is Ed Thorough, grey hair and dark beard, beer gut pushing out through the black polo shirt he always wears over the black jeans he always wears. Standard of dress is a moot point in the office and produces a fair percentage of complaints from the public, but black polo shirt and jeans are all Ed ever wears and will ever wear. Nobody, not even the top dogs, would fuck with Ed. He is at the same grade as Henry and Dave and all, but he answers to nobody. Fuck with Ed at your peril. If, on the other hand, you want something done, a bit of rough stuff to persuade a toerag to cough or someone to drag him on to a plane while turning a deaf ear to pleas for asylum . . . then Ed's your geezer. Ed cuts corners, but he gets results.

'He's not fucking going anywhere,' says Dave reassuringly. 'Not this duffer. He's a knock-off. Stone-cold refusal.'

'You've refused him, then?' asks Ed.

'Not yet. I was waiting for you to have a look at it. Get a second opinion,' says Dave. 'It's got to be duff,' he adds quietly, furrowing his brow as he picks it up again. 'Don't like this stitching. Someone's been fucking about with it. Bending it back,' he adds, bending it back.

Ed takes it off him and begins his inspection. He is turning the pages quickly at first, then slowly, then quickly again. Ed knows exactly what he is looking for. He breathes heavily through his nose as he inspects, bending back the spine once more for good measure, as he has to do. He holds it up to let the artificial light pass through it, then pulls it down at an angle to see the light bounce off it. Ed has his long, yellowed fingers in many pies, but forgery expert is very much his preferred mantle.

'What's the scrote want?' asks Ed, voice deep with experience.

'Transit,' explains Dave.

'Onward ticket?'

'Yes,' admits Dave.

'For when?' asks Ed, scraping away at the pages with his thumb.

'Tomorrow,' says Dave, worried now. If proceeding within twenty-four hours and in possession of an onward ticket, most visa nationals can benefit from a waiver.

'H'm,' says Ed. 'Sorry, Dave, mate. There's nothing wrong with it.'

Dave is crestfallen. 'I thought maybe the embossing—'

'It's not great,' says Ed, 'but it's as good as you're going to get. Quality of issue is so iffy. He probably got it out of some mud hut in the fucking jungle. But you'll have to give him the benefit of the doubt.'

He hands the passport to Dave, who looks as if he might cry.

'It is him, innit?' asks Ed. The question is not unusual, suggesting that although the passport is genuine, it may be in the possession of a *Double Gloucester* – an impostor.

Dave's eyes light up. 'I was wondering about that,' says Dave.

Ed rolls his eyes at Dave's sloppiness. *Fucking useless*, the gesture says.

'Should we?'

Ed snatches back the passport and shoves it into the rear pocket of his jeans. He leads Dave out of the office and out through the big black door on to the arrivals control beyond.

Xiao slides the bolt through the lock and turns into the tiny toilet space. Reaching into the inside pocket of his sports jacket, he pulls out the envelope containing his travel documents. Immediately, he begins ripping up his ticket and throws it down the toilet, as he was told to do. Now they would have no way of knowing which plane he was arriving off. Secondly, he begins to destroy the Portuguese passport saying he was born in Macao, starts by ripping back the plastic over the photograph and removing the picture that the forger put there. Dropping his likeness into the small steel sink, he sets fire to it with his lighter, putting a plastic cup over the flame to stop any smoke alarm from going off. He then tears the passport into tiny shreds and watches as his short-term identity, valid for one journey only, flushes away in the blue water.

Next, dropping to his haunches, he sets about removing the wastepaper bin that is set in the cabinet underneath the sink. One, two firm pulls and it comes away. He rummages among the crumpled paper towels until he touches the rectangular package wrapped in black plastic put there for him by the stewardess.

He opens it. It contains another passport, Chinese this time, one which bears his real name. This is the passport he is supposed to hand to the white-haired immigration officer, the one who is waiting for him and who will make the swap . . .

There's something else in the package and Xiao gently pulls it out.

A flick-knife. His weapon of choice. For settling scores . . .

Henry arrives at his locker and opens it. Reaching in, he pulls out his own personal landing stamp, flipping off the top to adjust the date from when he last used it. Three weeks fly by on the rubber rollers of the stamp's interior. Henry closes the locker and makes his way out of the room towards the duty office and the daily ritual of stamping on. Henry carries the stamp by its bulbous handle, dangling it between two of his fingers with his palm turned upwards. Its handle is thickly covered with Sellotape, as advised by a doctor after a visit for recurring eczema between the fingers. Henry told the doctor that he was a librarian to explain his need for a stamp. The doctor was Indian, and Henry thought it better not to tell him exactly how he made a living.

The good thing about Henry's stamp is that, thanks to a small, strategically placed strip of tape, its number (every stamp has its own number, in Henry's case 189) never comes out when he stamps a passport, so nothing can ever be traced to him. In the climate of fear that Terminal C managers like to foster, the doctoring of stamps for the purposes of anonymity is common practice. If you stamp the wrong passport and they find out about it, you're on your own. Hence the Sellotape.

Cover your back, cover your back

The carpet beneath him as he walks is brown and stained. He looks down as if it is the source of the terrible musty smell that lingers everywhere, knowing that the smell is a combination of a number of things, not least the cheap fresheners the cleaners pollute with and the burned pasta twirls of dust that dangle from the air-conditioners.

Around the duty office door, a queue of officers is forming, all armed with stamps like Henry's. This is the 'F' shift, the two-'til-niners, of whom Henry is one, all stamping on. Henry joins the back of the queue, colleagues who have completed their task passing by the other way. He nods in recognition to one or two.

There is a tap on Henry's shoulder. He turns around. It's Ronan Docherty, a short, stocky Ulsterman with a healthy contempt for immigration in general and Terminal C in particular.

'What happened to your hair?'

Henry ruffles it again.

'Just something to do.'

'Son of Ed Thorough,' says Ronan.

'Shit. I never thought of that.'

'Anyway, you look like a tosser,' Ronan opines, closing the subject there. 'You heard about—?'

'Onions?'

'Yeah,' says Ronan, eyes wide. 'Bloody brilliant, so it is.' There's nothing Ronan likes more than a bit of gossip.

'It's true he was suspended?'

Ronan nods.

'Who was he bringing in? You got a theory yet?' Ronan is famous for having theories.

'Better than theories,' Ronan says, lowering his voice now. 'You know there's a mate of my brother's who's an airport copper? He told me – strictly off the record this is, mind – that they found his stamp number in the passport of a bloke who was picked up for selling smack in Chinatown.'

'So? Christ knows how many crims you and I have landed without knowing who they were.'

'Yeah, but this guy's got a residency stamp. When the Old Bill try to get his Home Office file, there isn't one. No trace of him ever making an application. All they've got is Onions' landing stamp in his passport.'

Henry nods, understanding now.

'Christ. Of all people. Was it a one-off or what?'

'Don't know. There's still going to be an inquiry. Management here wanted to keep it in-house and pass on their findings to the police. Because it was Onions and he had his tongue up their arses, they were making noises about innocent until proved, blah blah. They would have covered it up, I reckon. But then he goes and pulls his own plug. The thing is,' he adds, 'the word is that he wasn't in it alone.'

'How do they know that?'

Ronan turns his lip.

'Well, it's just talk. You know what this office is like.'

Henry scratches his head.

'Still, bad business,' Ronan says.

'Bad business,' agrees Henry.

They are nearing the head of the queue. Henry is dismayed to see Ralph Hammond leaning on a filing cabinet next to the stamping-on book, inspecting everyone's stamps. Ralph Hammond is a Chief Immigration Officer, the grade above Henry and the others. He sports the tweed jacket and corduroy trousers he always wears and is tapping a plastic biro against the top of the filing cabinet in tempo *molto irritanto.* He has no wife, as he is married to his job and bigamy is against the immigration rules.

Quickly, before Hammond sees him, Henry pulls the strip of Sellotape off the bottom of his stamp. Reaching the front, he steps up, avoiding eye contact.

'Mr Brinks,' Hammond sneers. 'Ready to work hard today?'

Henry says nothing but directs his attention to the register, locating the space allocated for his stamp to leave its mark. He bounces his stamp off the ink pad and then on to the book, pushing hard so that the number will come out as well as the date. He stands back.

'Do it again,' says Hammond.

'What's wrong with it?' says Henry.

'That eight looks like a six. Do it again.'

Henry looks down at the impression he has left. The eight looks like an eight. He tuts and goes through the procedure again.

'That will have to do,' Hammond says, the erectile tissue of his authority swelling to magnificent proportions. 'Don't push your luck.' Hammond is famous for his vague threats. And for walking like there's a carrot up his arse. And for being an utter . . .

Henry walks back down the corridor, reattaching the Sellotape strip, his heart finding new subterranean quarters to lurk in.

Ronan catches up with him. 'I didn't tell you the most interesting thing about this whole Onions business.'

'Which is?'

'That Onions kills himself but leaves no note, nothing.'

'I guess a lot of suicides don't leave notes.'

'Aw, c'mon, man. We're talking about Onions, the king of the pointless memo. The guy once wrote a three-page essay on the most efficient use for the little circles of paper that are left after you've used a hole punch. He probably wrote a letter of apology every time he farted. If he killed himself, he wrote a goodbye letter.'

Henry smiles ruefully. 'So you're saying he didn't kill himself? That's your theory?' he asks, rolling his eyes.

'I'm not saying that. What I'm saying is that the letter was there and that it was taken.'

'What the hell for?'

'Incriminates somebody else, maybe. I don't know. But if that letter turns up—' He sits back, puffing out his cheeks '—boom!'

Henry laughs. 'Boom?'

'Boom!' nods Ronan as they enter the staff room.

The Tannoy speaker, fixed high on the wall, spits. *'All IOs to the control. All IOs to the control . . .'*

Slowly the inhabitants of the room drag themselves up and slide out, landing stamps at the ready. Henry follows behind.

He is the last out of the door, but he does not leave the rest room empty. Sitting tight, a study in obliviousness to the activity around him, sits Roger Thorne. Roger is an IO too, nominally equivalent to Henry and all the others, but different rules apply to him. Roger has more years of service under his belt than Henry has had birthdays, and that counts for a lot. He operates on a mysterious, rarefied level. Like Ed Thorough, he is untouchable; no chief or inspector would dare to cross him. Unlike Ed, however, Roger chooses not to dirty his hands with the vulgar business of passengers, tickets, forgeries and the like. The idea of Roger, in the Armani suit he always wears, with his sculpted hair, actually asking anybody in his delicate Scottish brogue how much money they had for their trip to Britain was beyond the pale. Where Ed Thorough is the master artisan, Roger is the dilettante, languid and inscrutable, an insurmountable obstacle of wilful idleness.

He has many admirers. In Roger and his kind, the lag philosophy has reached its Darwinian apotheosis – he has evolved into a hyper-efficient lag, raking in maximum earnings for minimum output, the minimum being, in this case, nil. His bearing implies that somehow, somewhere on the aesthetic plane, he is fundamental to the correct running of the whole immigration operation (and how he loves that word, 'operation'), that he is part of an invisible fabric that binds everything together. He sits with a small star chamber of cronies on a number of committees, all designated mysterious acronyms and secretive purpose. Roger gently reminds those who would spar with him of his contacts, contacts with other government agencies, contacts with airlines, other contacts he will not discuss other than to let it be known they exist. He ventures out occasionally to meet certain flights, usually from the Gulf, not to see the passengers off them but to schmooze with the airline reps or some member of the crew. A kiss on each cheek, an intimate clinging of hands, hushed words. In this way, Roger runs his lucrative little side-operation, importing gifts for resale without the tedium of Customs interference. Carpets from Constantinople, as he insists on calling it, mysteriously finding their way into the corner of the forgery room, four at a time, then disappearing for good. The carefully wrapped artworks bearing exhortations in the Cyrillic alphabet to treat carefully never hang around for long. Then there are the foodstuffs, especially around Christmas, the boxes of Turkish delight, sold on at giveaway prices to the chosen few, like the crates of tinned caviar, the country of origin always, for some reason, scorched off the wooden exterior.

Roger is important in the received wisdom Henry knows better than to question, or to trust. The culture of the old lag persists and is condoned by the senior ranks. The risks of rocking the boat are grave. Henry, with five years in the job, cannot hope to be in their number, with the privilege it affords. Nor, however, is he junior enough to be excused as being a sprog.

Neither lag nor sprog. A terrible limbo.

So Roger sits, an open file of Home Office notices in front of him, actively doing nothing, eyes following passers-by, occasionally sweeping back his combed flop of black hair. He's on his fourth marriage, to an Indian woman who had previously been an illegal and whose case file was mistakenly put into his pigeonhole. Glancing through it, he took a shine to her passport photograph and the rest is history . . . well, that's the story. Anyway, she did represent a change in tradition for she doesn't work at Terminal C, as all his previous wives have done. Two of them, Carol and Sylvia, both still walk the corridors here, and both still carry his name and his Child Support cheques. Although they speak to each other, they never speak to Roger.

As Henry passes, Roger yawns and stretches. Henry reaches the great black door and pulls it open.

Sunday, he reminds himself. Double time.

Xiao stands still, but he's moving. The long conveyor drags him from the arrival gates, along the seemingly endless corridors of Terminal C to the immigration hall and his appointment. Around him, others aren't moving fast enough, so they walk, the plastic wheels of their luggage squealing against the textured rubber of the travolator. Xiao, however, is content to be carried along, his one leather holdall resting between his feet.

The knife he keeps tucked inside the waistband of his jeans. Arms at his side, he feels reassured by its bulk in gentle contact with his wrist.

Up ahead, he can see where the travolator comes to an end and lazy Americans complain about having to carry their luggage again. A sign tells him in English, which he understands, the direction of Passport Control.

He goes over his instructions.

Look out for the white hair . . .

The wall of desks stands ahead. Forty desks, grey and squat, on sentry duty. Shabby now, wearing the scars of the long battle; corners chipped off, barriers hanging limply off their hinges, some lurching to one side. Weather-beaten but unbowed they stand, the last line of defence.

Behind the line on the wrong side, a few scattered souls, mostly black-faced, sit and await an invisible judgement, wait for the double-headed coin to drop.

Henry walks towards the desks, keeping on this side of the line, the side of world-weary indignation. He walks past the smoked glass of the raised watchhouse overlooking the desks. CHIEF IMMIGRATION OFFICER says a sign on the front in blue with a proud crest above it, the same crest (lion, unicorn, *Dieu et mon droit*, the full monty) that graces the front of every officer's leather warrant card holder. Henry's shame dictates that his warrant never comes out of his back pocket. Others wear theirs freely, heartily strung around their necks, waving them furiously to get ten per cent off a coffee in the departures lounge or, legend has it, a free Indian meal anywhere in West London.

Out here, in the dark hangar of the arrivals hall, where

natural light is unwelcome by virtue of being natural, Sunday afternoon will come down to one thing.

Only one.

Refugees.

This is not accident; Sunday is the cheapest day for airport space and is favoured by airlines that specialise in trafficking the dispossessed, otherwise known as scrotes, toerags, etc. This afternoon will, like all Sunday afternoons, see their ranks swell exponentially until almost every seat on the control will be filled. Already, a large group of Salvadors are shuffling out of the Port Medical Inspector's office.

Salvador. Salvador Dali. Somali.

These are the first wave and have just had their mandatory X-rays for TB, a disease alive and well in the East End of London

The row of desks is filling up as IOs drift out, looking for a good spot, not too close to an offensive colleague. Henry wanders along the line of desks, moving into a seat flanked by two empty neighbours. Behind him, the giant boards announcing arrivals whir up the bad news like a flock of startled birds beating a retreat.

Prrrrrrrrrrrrrrrrt

In the distance, the first passengers dribble down the ramp that leads into the hall. They begin to be distributed by the presenters, half-blind old Sikh men hired at a pittance to control the front of the queue and send them to the first available desk.

The first stamps crash down – *boombang* – on the first passports. The act of stamping is one of defiance. This is how it's always been done, with a forearm-quivering impact, not a pissy little push. No concession to repetitive strain injury here, wrists and elbows habitually sacrificed to the gesture of *granting leave to enter.*

Each stamp bears date, location (London Terminal C) and

individual stamp number. A flange at the top contains the legend SIX MONTHS' LEAVE TO ENTER. EMPLOYMENT PROHIBITED. This is the most common stamp, given to nearly all visitors. It is added by rolling the stamp forward after collision with the passport. This action gives it the name by which it is generally known. The *roll.*

P*rrrrrrrrrrrrrrrrrrrrrrrrrrrrrrrt*

Boom

Prrrt

Bang

Henry wonders again, as he does every day, what the hell he is doing here. *How did I end up here?* There's the bank loan, of course, still paying for the ill-fated video production company he had started with a friend. The £15,000 his grandmother had left him in her will was all gone. All those weddings he never got paid for filming. He never sees that friend now. Nobody here at Terminal C knows about this horribly underprepared venture. At the rate he is paying off what he owes the bank, he still needs to do two years at the airport, then he will have to carry on saving for at least another eighteen months before he can seriously consider leaving. He just doesn't have the luxury of being able to walk out, especially when he knows that having 'Immigration Officer' on your CV renders you virtually unemployable anywhere else.

He blinks slowly, asking himself the question again.

Why, of all jobs, did it have to be this one? Why did it have to be a job that sapped the very life out of you, that was designed to crush your self-esteem flat? Was this the professional life he had gone through university for, sitting, stamping passports, when so many of his friends had exciting, challenging, creative employment? But education and the Immigration Service are uncomfortable bedfellows. The increasingly high level of qualification among new recruits is something deeply resented by the old guard, and here, in this Luddite, reactionary corner of public service, it merits no respect. The old lag system, a bloody-minded anachronism sanctioned from the very top, is the way that clever dicks like Henry are kept in check, taught their place, even humiliated when necessary. There's no bucking the trend.

And all around him, the beneficiaries of this perverse order go about their business.

Take Dick Foster, heavy-jowled Glaswegian, six or seven desks down. He always sits a long way from anyone else, which is just as well. Dick Foster is possibly the most unpopular person working at Terminal C in what is a competitive area for distinction. His status is in part due to the stench of grease that surrounds him, but his talent for being objectionable would set him apart at an Orange Order stag party. He was transferred to Terminal C from Terminal B as a disciplinary measure after head-butting a Canadian diplomat and calling him a 'moose-fucker'.

It is hard to get sacked from the Immigration Service.

Now he's got two South American passengers at his desk. Henry recognises their blue passports as Argentinian. Foster takes one and looks at its reverse side. Henry knows what's coming. Argentinian passports bear a crude map on their backs, which incorporates a small group of islands on the eastern coast. Dick sniffs and points them out.

'What's that, aye? What are these islands here?'

The couple are embarrassed, smile awkwardly. 'They are islands off our coast,' says the man, thin, well groomed.

'Oh, yeah? What they called?'

The couple glance at one another, as if about to take a ride on an unfinished roller-coaster.

'We call them Malvinas,' says the young woman. 'They are very close to our country.'

Dick slams the two passports on to the desk. 'Falklands,' he says, rolling his tongue along his teeth. 'Falklands.'

The young couple look down.

'Say it,' says Dick Foster.

'I'm sorry?'

'Say it. *Fork-lands. Fork-lands.*'

'Fawlaw,' mutters the woman, nudging her partner.

'Fawbs,' he adds, deeply ashamed.

'There,' says Dick, crashing his stamp down twice – *boom-bangaboombang*. 'That wasn't so hard. I'm finished wi' ya,' he adds, flinging the passports back.

Depressed by his own resignation to this kind of behaviour as much as the behaviour itself, Henry watches them go, trying to underplay their humiliation. There is no doubt that five years here have coarsened Henry, rendered him more cynical than he would ever have wished to become, but at least he isn't like Foster; at least he still has that much humanity. He wonders what Dick was like when he started his 'career', probably twenty years ago. Is Henry looking at a picture of himself in a decade's time when he sees Foster or Ed Thorough or Roger Thorne?

Christ!

The first buffet of Terminal C depression slams into him. It is a unique sensation, like being cored.

. . . White hair . . .

Away to his left is Ed Thorough, standing with Dave Niblo. Facing them is the holder of the passport from Niger, watching as they perpetrate further assault on his travel document.

'Is this you?' says Ed to the man.

'It is me,' says the man. He wears a snot-green shirt with billowing sleeves, grey trousers with silver flashes and sandals. 'It is I,' he repeats with a laugh suggesting he is amused, knowing that the officers are playing a joke on him. It is a tactic that Henry has seen used before, and he recognises the reaction of someone who's been rumbled. Ed moves nearer and brings the passport right up to his face, glancing first at the picture, then at the man, then at the picture again. Dave leans forward on tiptoes, straining to make the same comparison.

'The ears are the giveaway,' says Ed. 'You can't change the shape of your ears. You see. Different shape. These ears here are squarer and smaller, the lobes are bigger. See?' Dave nods. 'Ears,' he says to the passenger. 'Your ears give you away, mate. These ears, here in the photo, they're not yours.'

'These my ears,' insists the man, fatally still behaving as if he were on a children's television show. Always better to get angry, go on the offensive.

Ed shakes his head. 'No, mate.'

Dave Niblo smiles, loving it.

'Not your ears,' Ed says. 'Not you.'

The man's behaviour veers suddenly towards the desperate. 'No,' he says, waving a long finger in Ed Thorough's face, not recommended practice. 'It is an old picture. My ears have changed since it was taken.'

'Changed?' asks Ed. 'Changed how?' Henry notices that, as he speaks, Thorough is looking away every few seconds, towards the entrance to the arrivals hall. As if he's expecting . . .

The man pulls at the lobe of his ear. 'They are different. I have grown since this photo.'

'But your ears have shrunk?' asks Ed, still watching as other passengers drift into the hall.

'They have shrunk because my head has grown.'

'I see.' Ed laughs, his concentration momentarily back. Dave laughs. The man starts to laugh too, thinking it is a good sign.

It is not a good sign. The man senses it, sniffs trouble on the wind and decides to change tack. He glances at them both, a sudden sorrow in his eyes.

'Please,' he says. 'You must help me. I cannot go back there. I am in . . .'

. . . *fear of my life*. Henry can mouth the words along with him, so familiar are they.

'Please,' continues the man. 'I am axing for poltic' 'sylo.'

Plan B. Dave groans and turns away. In a gesture clearly washing his hands of any further responsibility, Ed Thorough lets out a whistle and hands the document to Dave. Ed doesn't touch refugees.

The door to the office opens.

'Ed,' shouts Roger Thorne.

'What is it?'

Roger puts his left hand to his ear in a lazy approximation of a telephone receiver.

'Who is it?'

Roger shrugs *how should I know?*

Ed looks at his watch, then across the hall again, apparently concerned.

'Shit,' he mutters, running a hand distractedly through his white mane before heading into the office to take the call.

Xiao enters the hall carefully. If he doesn't see White Hair immediately, he will stall, stop to tie his shoelaces, give himself the chance to look around.

But he can hardly miss the unnatural shock of blond in the middle of the row of desks, younger than he expected . . .

Xiao moves in.

Henry looks on as Dave vents his fury.

'You,' he says to the small-eared man, 'are a scrote.'

'Thank you, sir,' replies his passenger.

Henry turns, ready to get off the desk.

From nowhere, there's someone in front of him.

A young Chinese male, nasty-looking bastard, staring back at him.

Henry jumps.

'Christ!' he says. 'You gave me a shock.'

No reply. Just a stare.

Looking around with a touch of panic, Henry sees the control starting to clear of his fellow officers. He chides himself for inadvertently making the most elementary error, one a sprog in his first month would be embarrassed at.

RULE NUMBER ONE:
Never,
Never,
NEVER
Take the Last Person Off a Flight
(Always Trouble)

The man's short hair stands brush-like atop his head, his posture betraying a strong, sinewy frame. He is wearing jeans, a white T-shirt underneath a grey double-breasted jacket, and is carrying a brown leather bag. He would look a right tit were it not for his mean, unrelenting gaze.

Henry responds with a parody of indifference, sniffing hard and asking for a passport with a sigh.

The man blinks slowly and drops a red passport on the desk. Henry notices a crude star-shaped tattoo scratched into the skin on the back of his hand. He cannot help feeling a little intimidated.

'Do you speak English?' he asks, pretending to yawn.

Obviously not.

Henry locates the passport photograph. The same face stares back at him, a little more hair, but the same tight neck, the same dead eyes. Henry looks at the details.

Name	**XIAO PING**
Date of Birth	**10/4/77**
Place of Birth	**Szechuan**

Passport issued only a week before. Henry flicks through the pages. No Julius. This means that tough guy in front of him is in trouble, as per Paragraph 24 of the Immigration Rules. Even if in transit, the Chinese are one of the few nationalities for which a visa is never waived.

'Visa?' says Henry to the man.

No reply. Just the steel-capped stare, drilling him through.

Henry feels a secret pleasure at the knowledge that he has the power to fuck up this arrogant little gook. Quickly he fills out Home Office form IS81, requiring him to submit to further examination, and slides it across the desk.

The gook looks down at it, then back at Henry.

Henry smiles and gives him a thumbs-down sign.

A muscle flicks in the gook's neck, his eyes give off something between a question and a death threat. Henry's pulse quickens a notch. He sets about putting the name into the suspect catalogue computer he has on the desk, a database of hundreds of thousands of names of 'interest'.

He presses RETURN.

WARNING, flashes the screen.

WARNING – VIOLENT

WARNING

WARNING – VIOLENT

WARNING

WARNING – VIOLENT

Henry rocks on his heels, feels the skin around his shoulder blades tighten.

WARNING

Nice one, Henry, he thinks. Of all the people you could have taunted, you had to choose a fully paid-up psycho.

VIOLENT

Dragging his eyes up, Henry points to the seats behind the gook and strains out another false yawn.

The man doesn't move.

WARNING – VIOLENT, Henry is reminded. He clears the computer screen.

He points to the seats behind the gook and strains out another false yawn. The man doesn't move, but instead flashes a look over Henry's shoulder.

Henry looks around.

It's Ed Thorough standing, watching. He doesn't want to be seen to back down, wouldn't want the likes of Thorough coming to bail him out. Turning back, he points to the seats again.

The Chinese glances across at Thorough, then double-takes, as if in realisation of something. He sits down.

Henry turns and heads towards the chiefies' watchhouse with the passport. He climbs the three steps that give access to it.

As usual, it is dark, lit only by a solitary Anglepoise and the radiation of computer screens. Chiefies seem to think this gives it the air of a high-tech centre of operations or the battle bridge of the SS *Enterprise*. Prolonged exposure can certainly bring on a bastard of a migraine.

Two chiefies in the watchhouse. There's Hammond, of course, hunched forward, tapping some memorandum with his pen as he reads it. And then there's the dreadful Sharon Barber, formerly Sharon Coates, formerly Sharon Dray, formerly Sharon . . . before Henry's time. Known as the Black Widow, she is on her third marriage, each one to fellow immigration personnel. This is, in itself, not unusual. What is generally thought to be unique, however, is her gradual progression up the career ladder in search of a mate. First, as a lowly IO of a few months' experience she had married Chief Immigration

Officer Dray. That didn't last long. She broke him like a stale breadstick and moved on to the next level and the tender mercies of Mr Coates, known affectionately as the Knife. During the tenure of this union, Sharon had achieved her own promotion and his rank became too close to her own for comfort. So she dumped the Knife, blunted now, for an Assistant Commissioner at headquarters named Barber. The joke is that he scuttles around blocking any further promotion for her just to keep their marriage intact. A nice thought, but for someone as ruthless as the Black Widow, the cobweb only takes you up.

As Henry enters, she is mouthing words from beneath a slagheap of make-up.

'I don't know what the fuck he's doing here,' she's saying. 'This is no place for a man who's mourning.'

'I would agree that he does seem to be bringing Edna to work with him,' says Hammond. Edna, presumably, being a corpse.

'That's it,' agrees Shazza. 'He's got to pull his weight. I haven't got time to carry him. Far too fucking busy. We're all far too fucking busy . . .'

A bereaved colleague will not occupy the conversation long. Tragedy stalks the Immigration Service, the chiefies and above especially, with remarkable regularity. Sudden bereavement, suicides, terminal illness, you name it. Henry appears to be alone in discerning this pattern. They are, of course, cursed – promotion comes with its own Faustian payback. You get what you deserve, he supposes.

Henry doesn't know about Hammond, but Sharon, for example, has definitely suffered at the hands of chiefy's curse. At a specialist nursing home somewhere in the country lies a son by her first marriage, a persistent vegetative following an assignation with a bag of glue. The only obvious effect of this tragedy are her occasional sadistic bouts of raffle-ticket selling around the office, from which nobody has ever won a prize.

Henry goes to one of the terminals and brings up the screen for recording a new case. He begins to tap in the passport details.

'I've got a Chinese, no visa,' he announces.

'What do you want? A medal?' spits Sharon.

'I'm just saying,' says Henry.

'I'm just saying,' she imitates in a high-pitched whine. 'I'm just saying.'

Henry enters the pertinent information and he presses RETURN, storing it in the computer's memory. An empty box at the bottom of the screen appears with the unique case number, X94153, which he writes on a yellow adhesive notelet he attaches to the passport front.

Henry doesn't hear Thorough come up the steps to the podium.

'What've you got there, then?' he asks, toning down the normal boom of his voice to a growling whisper.

His silent arrival, not to mention his unprecedented interest in anything Henry has ever done, is disconcerting. It makes Henry shiver.

'I, er . . . nothing much. Chinese, no visa. Nothing special.'

'Can I have a look at the doc?' asks Ed, pointing to the passport in Henry's hand.

'Sure. It says on the computer that he's—'

Ed stops him with a shake of the head and a finger put to his lips. Henry furrows his brow. Ed nods towards the chiefics, with a look that says they are not to be trusted. The insecure part of Henry's character is consoled by this token acceptance into Thorough's circle of confidence, although there is a threat in his eyes as he looks at Henry.

'Just give me the passport,' says Ed.

Henry gives it to him. Ed sees the yellow notelet on the front of the passport.

'This the case reference?'

'Yes,' says Henry.

Thorough lets out a sigh through his nose. Henry smells the booze on his breath. Ed turns to Hammond, who has his back to them, still intent in his reading. For some reason he chooses to bypass Sharon, who is closer by. Henry puts this down to male chauvinism, although there is always the possibility of a particular antipathy dating back centuries, maybe the result of a brief romance that curdled after a couple of upright shags in the forgery room.

'Ralph,' he says. 'I'm going to take on this Chinese case. Just a no visa.'

Henry is surprised at Thorough's interest in such a routine case, but at the same time pleased about dodging even the vaguest threat of violence. He's got the credit for putting the gook on the computer and it will count towards his yearly total of refusals, which could do with a late boost.

'Any particular reason?' This is Sharon.

'I'm doing an intelligence exercise on Chinese arrivals, if you must know.'

'First I've heard of it,' says Sharon.

Ed shrugs.

'No reason why you should hear of it. Bob Gascoigne asked me to do it.'

Bob Gascoigne. Bob the Bitch. The Port Commissioner, top dog at Terminal C, three grades above Henry, and a fully accredited puppy-strangler. Satan, they say, is a Bob Gascoigne worshipper.

By invoking his name, Ed raises the stakes. Although in the grade above Ed, Sharon is still seriously junior to him in terms of years served. It is a common trick of the Bitch to undermine the chiefies by ignoring them in the chain of command. Sharon twists her mouth but adds nothing. Not that Ed is paying her any attention.

'Ralph?' he repeats. 'Ralph? That OK?'

Slowly, Hammond turns at the shoulders and gives a curiously understated nod. Having got the result he wanted, Ed leaves, taking just a moment to look Henry up and down. Henry watches Ed through the smoked glass as he moves towards the gook, whistles at him and gestures for him to sit down at the far end of the control. Then, leaving him there, Thorough walks away back in the direction of the arrival gates. Perhaps he's going to meet somebody he knows arriving off a flight, or more likely popping down for a swift two or three in the departures bar with one of his umpteen airport cronies. Unlike junior IOs, who have to make their whereabouts known at all times, Ed's class can come and go as they please. But no, he takes a turn into the public toilets, almost bumping into a uniformed pilot coming out. Maybe the office khazi has flooded, which seems to happen on a weekly basis. Or maybe he's gone to have a root around to look for some of the narcotics that you can usually find there, dumped by backpackers or in some cases couriers who just bottle it at the last minute.

It's finders keepers in the public bogs. Perk of the job.

'Funny,' Henry mutters.

Hammond drops his pen on the waist-high counter in irritation.

'Haven't you got something to do?' he snaps.

Henry trots down the steps from the watchhouse, hands in pockets, and back into the office.

Dave Niblo is back in the same seat, still poking around with the Niger passport, hacking away with a pin at the photograph now.

'Yeah, it's genuine. Of course, the quality of the issue is

crap.' He slaps it down on the desk. 'What d'you expect from these fucking jungle bunnies?'

Daniella looks up from her copy of *Marie-Claire*. 'Dave,' she says, by way of a gentle reprimand. 'You can't say that.'

Dave makes a face.

'Anyway, he – *he* – is as duff as fuck.' He groans again. 'I can't believe he's gone PA.'

PA. Political asylum. Two letters that hang heavy in the air at Terminal C, dropping like a grand piano from a skyscraper, fugging the atmosphere as relentlessly as the air-conditioners. Two letters which signify a working process so ultimately futile as to render one numb to the case of the most desperate refugee – although that, the word refugee, is seldom used. People who arrive at Terminal C in their dozens, even hundreds on some days, are *asylum seekers*. To call them refugees is heresy, as it implies an unacceptable level of sympathy within a system designed to flush the majority out as economic migrants.

Anybody who makes or is interpreted to have made a claim to political asylum is entitled to have that claim initially considered. Most have no passport, no money, no ticket, no English, only their purpose apparent.

Then there are the punters like Dave Niblo's, playing his joker. Going to plan B, his fallback option should his attempt to gain entry as an impostor fail, as it has done. Even Henry has some sympathy for Dave here, because it means that all the work he's done so far – the forgery report, the almost complete case notes, the arrangements for removal that he has just completed – count for nothing. Nobody likes to have their time wasted.

'Fucking duffer,' he mutters to himself. 'Just stick him on the fucking plane, eh? What if I never heard him say anything about PA, eh? His word against mine? Fuckin' scrote.'

Henry knows that, coming from Dave, this is an empty threat. But there are old lags, always allergic to asylum work (*'not real immigration work, not what I joined the service for . . .'*), who openly boast about forcibly removing passengers of the wrong skin group amid pleas for asylum . . . *sorry, no asylum today . . . no, asylum full up this year . . . all council houses gone . . . asylum, what is?* . . . Dave loves these stories, never doubting their veracity, but doesn't have the bottle, or the seniority, to get away with it. His small-eared impostor has gone PA and that was that. After all, it's Sunday afternoon. Everybody is going to be drinking from the bottomless well of Fugee before the afternoon is out. Except for Roger Thorne, who stays where he is, muttering into the telephone now, clocking up the double time.

'I'm serious,' he's saying. 'I'm serious about it . . . No, I am . . . I told him if I was overlooked for promotion one more time, I would be forced to take measures. He knew it was no empty threat, he knew, all right . . . Well, I gave them a fair warning . . .'

The Tannoy snaps on again and Sharon's voice crackles instructions. '*We have Royal Arabian Airways passengers coming into the hall,*' it rants. '*The Royal Arabian is in the hall. I want every officer out. And I mean every officer. That means all the Bs and all the Fs. And that means now.*'

People trudge out again, leaving Roger behind. Not even the Black Widow would dare to disturb Roger.

Three flights are coming in on the Royal Arabian's tail, heralding a long stretch.

Two of the three come from the Middle East, but are notable for having East African connections. This gives the legion of refusal-happy IOs, the head-hunters, something to look forward to. They come out first, sniffing the dirty air for something to *knock off*, someone to *bounce.* Henry sees Daniella's boyfriend, the appalling Paul Speerpoint, blond hair gelled back, in the black blazer he always wears, one corner of his mouth turned up in a smirk of anticipation, hurry out to a desk further down the row. He'll have one before too long, some poor sod will find himself refused, stitched up like a kipper. Henry prays that he gets nothing, still afraid after five years of confrontation, still afraid of making accusations he can't back up with fact, afraid of making a mistake, afraid of *it*. *It* being the moment when it gets nasty, when you come face to face with the passenger who was born half a world away solely for the purpose of fucking you over. All you're really doing is hanging around, marking time, humming the mantra *cover your back, cover your back, cover your back*.

Waiting for *it*. If you haven't met it already . . .

At least he doesn't get the dreams any more, the ones where he's drowning in passports, choking on them . . .

Prrrrrrrrrrrrrrrrrrrrrrrrrrrrrrrrrrrrrrrrrrrt

Henry notices Speerpoint watching the queue carefully. He has his arm raised, telling the presenters not to send anybody. *Not yet, not yet, not yet, no, don't want her, no, no, I'll pass on him and go for the big prize* . . . A young African male, possibly Kenyan, comes to the front of the line. He drops his arm. *NOW!* . . . Speerpoint is playing the queue, waiting for the one he wants. Henry plays the queue in his own way, but always with the opposite intention, always to avoid what looks like a case. If he doesn't fancy someone, he holds the passenger he's got, asking a trivial question or making a joke until another desk is free.

Boombang

Bangboom

Boom

Henry watches the young man pass him on the way to Speerpoint's desk, with his shiny suit (way too big), his cheap briefcase (obviously empty) and his nervous gait. A lamb to the slaughter. Forget the Western pretensions. Better to dress up like something out of *Zulu*. He's refused before Speerpoint even asks him a question.

Looking down to the far end of the control, Henry sees the no-visa Xiao seated on the last of the plastic seats, just sitting there, looking around, taking it all in, surprisingly unperturbed. Something about him, something ugly, makes it hard for Henry to take his eyes off him . . .

Dave Niblo takes the desk next to Henry. Now that his case has gone PA, he has no interest in it and has fobbed it off on somebody else. He points to the African as he passes on his way.

'Look. He's wearing his refusal shoes,' says Dave.

Henry simply nods with a wry smile. Refusal shoes, a long-running joke among IOs. Stone-cold knock-offs have a habit of turning up in garishly inappropriate footwear: spats, patent-leather brogues, sneakers with flashing lights around the perimeter of the sole. Henry leans over the desk to get a decent look as the knock-off walks by. If he has ever seen refusal shoes, they are these: a pair of white plastic boat shoes sporting oversized tassels.

Anything with tassels and you're asking for trouble.

Every few seconds, Henry sends a glance across at Xiao. Something is nagging him, a foreboding. Maybe he shouldn't have just let Thorough steamroller him like that . . .

Quickly, the hall begins to fill up, the air is violent with stamping *boombang*, shouting. It is a situation lurching on the cusp of *boom* chaos *bang*, its smell drawing the CIOs out from the anonymity of the watchhouse to push the queues through quicker, which is their true priority, the integrity of the immigration control translated instantly to *just worry about the darkies*.

BoomBoomBoom
Bangbang, Boom
Boom
Prrrrrrrrrrrrrrrrrrrrrrrrrrrrrrrrrrrt

Looking down the line of desks, Henry sees heads bobbing

back and forth like hens in a battery farm. 'Customers' slither between the desks and on, down the escalators to the baggage hall.

Boom

Bang

Boom Bang

Half of the desks are full now, but the population of the hall is growing faster than it can be filtered through by the staff available. The queue lengthens. Tempers shorten. Anxiety courses through the fibres of the ugly purple carpet and gushes down from the black space above the metal ceiling grids. As it's Sunday and everyone is on double time, the departmental budget can't stretch to any extra staff to cope with the extra passengers.

'How long? . . .' *Boom*

BangboomBoom

'How long? . . .'

Prrrrrrrrrrrt *Boombangabangabang*

'How long? . . .'

Henry notices the model for this season's refusal shoes, who has been sat down by Speerpoint. He is inspecting the Home Office form IS81 he has been given, informing him that he is a passenger who is subject to further examination and liable to be detained. His demeanour suggests that there is still hope of a positive outcome. But when Speerpoint has your trouser leg between his perfect teeth, there's no hope.

A few more passengers pass through Henry's desk. His questions cursory, his mind in neutral, he's unable to take his eye off Xiao. Something not right . . .

The desk next to Henry's right has been empty. It is filled now by a hefty presence. Henry turns and sees the distinctive figure of Guldeep Singh, dressed, as ever, in silk shirt with embroidered, Vegas-period Elvis collar and leather waistcoat.

He is wearing a green turban today. 'What fucking rubbish have we got here, then?' he asks Henry.

'Dunno,' says Henry.

Guldeep is your classic poacher-turned-gamekeeper, as ethnic IOs are known. His contempt for blacks is legend, and when he can be bothered to do anything at all he usually goes after them. He plays the queue like a Stradivarius until a proud-looking African husband and wife are sent in the direction of his desk. Henry reckons they are probably resident in Britain; they have an air of familiarity with the Terminal C arrivals hall.

'What have we got here, then?' mutters Guldeep as they approach, still out of earshot. 'Fucking chocolate Family Robinson.'

Prrrrrrrrrrrrrrrrrrrrrrrrrrrrrrrrrrrrrrrrrrrrrrrrrrrtt

The boards have clicked up the arrival of Air Canton from Beijing. Looking back across at Xiao, still sitting there, Henry notices the slightest of changes in his bearing, a little shuffle in his seat, the first hint of discomfort.

Behind him, Henry sees Thorough emerge from the lavatories, looking a little self-conscious. He's carrying an envelope, a manila envelope, A5 size, holding it to his side, the side facing away from the control.

Don't remember him carrying that, thinks Henry.

At the other end of the control, a man is walking behind the line of desks, handing a sheet of paper to every IO. Henry recognises him as one of the team of Special Branch Officers posted to Terminal C who occasionally interrupt their three-year drinking contest to intercept a few known criminals. The sheet of paper will have a name on it. One to look out for. Miss him and you'd be in trouble.

By now, Guldeep is laying into the coloured family, who are, as Henry thought, UK residents. Despite their impeccable clothing and obviously Western demeanour, or perhaps because of it, Guldeep is out for blood.

'So you live in Bath, do you?' he asks, raising an eyebrow.

'That is correct.'

'And what do you do?'

'In what sense?'

Guldeep leans forward over his large stomach. 'What . . . is . . . your . . . job . . .?'

'I'm a physician, and there is no need to use that tone of voice.'

Guldeep tuts and sighs and rolls his eyes in a pantomime of impatience. 'You just appear to be having difficulty understanding my questions for someone who claims to have been here for twenty years.'

'Your diction is not clear.'

'I take offence at that remark,' Guldeep says, nicely trumping them with his own little race card.

'This is absurd. Ask your questions so that we can go.'

'You may go when I give you permission.'

The doctor's wife, silent until now, lets out a groan of pained amusement.

'Is something funny?' snaps Guldeep.

'You are, you stupid little man,' says she, to her husband's annoyance.

Ouch. Henry winces. That's it, he thinks. They'll be here for the next twenty minutes, answering questions about their history and the colour of the buses in Bath. Jokey tradition dictates this is the question that a doubtful resident is always asked: the colour of the buses. Henry has considered compiling a manual, working title *The Stone-Cold Duffer's Guide to Provincial British Bus Colourings*. He reckons he would clean up.

Passengers continue to come at him in their tedious variety. A couple of fat Kuwaiti women drift through Henry's desk, pretending to be some kind of royalty. If they were really that important, Henry knows they'd be down in the Davenport Suite for VIPs, stuffing themselves on complimentary biscuits and nicking the ashtrays. He doesn't ask them to remove their shawls, as this always causes trouble. They have actually gone to the lengths of hiding their passport photographs behind strips of opaque Sellotape. This modesty seems slightly out of synch with their flurry of questions about tax-free shopping at Harrods, to which Henry has no answers.

Bang, his stamp booms down, marking time.

Prrrrrrrrrboomrrrrrrrrbangboomrrrrrrrrrbangabangrrrrrrt

'How long? . . .'

' . . . Show me how much money you have . . .'

' . . . No return ticket? No return ticket? How strange . . .'

' . . . How many days? Yes or no? . . .'

' . . . You're lying to me. Why are you lying to me? . . .'

Bang

Bang

Bang

' . . . That's a long time for a holiday, isn't it? . . .'

'You're close friends? . . . Just how close exactly? . . .'

' . . . You think this is enough money? . . .'

'Take a seat, please . . .'

Prrrrrrrrrrbangboomt

To his right, the coloured residents are still at Guldeep's desk and beginning to look a little worried. In front of them, Guldeep is staring avidly at two American green cards.

'It says here that you became residents of the United States three years ago. Yes?'

'That's when the papers came through.'

'And you were already in the country at that time?'

'Yes,' comes the reply, with a 'so what' shake of the head.

'So how long is it since you lived here?'

'I am a resident here.'

'I'll repeat the question. How long is it since you actually lived here?'

Husband and wife confer. 'Three years,' he offers.

Ouch again. One of the dustiest corners of the Act is the little rule about residents having to return within two years. Almost unknown to the public, it is a head-hunter's dream.

Guldeep goes in for the kill.

'Let me go over what you've told me. You haven't worked in this country for three years, since when you have been resident in America. You don't have any property or family here at this time. Is that correct?'

'Yes, but there is a British residency stamp in my p—'

With the remonstration still in their throats, he quickly flings both passports down and rolls them. *Boom boom.*

'Those are visitors' stamps,' he explains.

'But I have residency in my passport.'

'Not any more. By giving you a visitor's stamp I have cancelled your residency. Good day,' he adds, handing the passports back. In the head-hunter's extensive repertoire, this is an elegant device; the satisfaction equivalent to a refusal without the tiresome paperwork.

The couple gasp and begin their inevitable recriminations. Henry loses interest.

The Special Branch Officer has reached Henry's desk. He slides a piece of paper from the pile he has on to the desk in front of Henry.

'Looking for someone off the Canton,' he explains.

Henry looks down and his throat goes dry.

XIAO PING CHN 10/4/77

A little too quickly, he looks back across to where the gook was sitting.

He's gone. The seat's empty.

Henry's eyes sweep the vicinity. No sign of—

There! A flash of grey jacket hurrying out of the hall from

the furthest corner, back towards the flight gates. And alongside, a tall figure, dressed in black, white-haired . . .

'I . . .'

He stops himself, the switch in his brain that governs *cover your back* flicks. He momentarily re-experiences the blend of conspiracy and threat he had felt as Thorough had put his finger to his lip in the watchhouse. There was something all-encompassing in Ed's advocacy of silence. Not even the Old Bill, *especially* not the Old Bill. Henry chooses to back off, keep his options open.

'You seen him?' asks Special Branch.

'No.' Henry shakes his head. 'Keep an eye out, though. What's he done?'

Special Branch puffs out his cheeks.

'What's he not done? Regular hard knock.'

'And, er . . .' Henry asks. 'What makes you think he's coming off the Canton?'

Special Branch looks puzzled at the question.

'He's Chinese, in he? It's a Chinese airline, innit?'

'Yeah, but, I mean, what if he's already come in on a different airline?'

Special Branch chuckles, shakes his head.

'Don't worry about that, son. They're not that clever.'

As Special Branch moves on, the black doctor from Bath is at Henry's desk.

'Do you work here?' he asks.

Never has Henry been asked a question so stupid, not even by a cross-eyed Kurdish goatherd.

'Yes,' he replies. He notices that Guldeep has made himself scarce.

'I'm made a written complaint,' says the doctor, waving a piece of paper.

'Whatever,' says Henry, eyes still trained on Special Branch.

'Who do I address it to?'

'What you say? . . . Oh, erm . . . Mr Hammond, Chief Immigration Officer.'

The doctor scribbles it down. 'There,' he says 'I've asked for a reply.'

Henry nods and takes it. The doctor and his wife pass through.

The Air Canton passengers pass through the control, slower than usual, Henry thinks, what with the ghost of Onions looming over them.

As they pass through, Special Branch paces behind, looking in vain for his quarry.

Things start to quieten a little, but Henry knows it's only a brief remission. He heads to the watchhouse, the doctor's complaint in hand.

Ronan intercepts him.

'Did you see that name Special Branch were giving out?'

'Yeah,' Henry replies hesitantly.

'I was chatting to him, pumping him for information, you know. You're not going to believe where they got that name.'

'Where?' asks Henry, feeling his chest tighten. He fears the worst, not even knowing what that might be.

'They found it in Onions' diary.'

'No,' says Henry, missing a breath. This is worse than worst. He's let go of a one-man Chinese crime wave who turns out to be connected to the suspicious death of a colleague. If anyone finds out . . .

Oh, Christ! A terrible thought hits him. He put the gook on the computer. It'll still be recorded there, with its unique case number and his own surname next to it as the reporting officer . . .

'Got to go,' he says, leaving Ronan standing.

Hammond is on the telephone with his back to Henry as he

clambers up the stairs to the watchhouse. He glances at the special screen there showing the last twenty cases that have arrived and been logged in. Each time there's a new one entered from anywhere in the building, the others get pushed down one.

Henry traces a finger down the list.

There it is. Three from the bottom.

XIAO PING **X94153** **BRINKS**

Down on the control, Henry sees that Special Branch has found his search fruitless. He turns away from the desks and – oh no! – comes towards the watchhouse.

Somewhere, another case is entered and Henry's name gets pushed down one. Only two more and the evidence will be gone.

But by now Special Branch is at the bottom of the short stairway.

Henry takes a step across to the nearest terminal. He has to enter another case to get his boy off.

He brings up the New Case programme.

The cursor flashes at a box entitled **MAIN NAME**.

Name? Name?

He taps in Ali and presses RETURN.

OTHER NAMES, the computer wants to know.

Baba. RETURN.

Special Branch is in the watchhouse now, waiting for Hammond to get off the phone . . .

No other cases have gone on. Still two from the bottom . . .

NATIONALITY

Nationality? Nationality? He can't think of one. Fuck-fuckfuckfuckfuck . . .

Hammond puts down the receiver.

'Yes?' he asks Special Branch.

'I just wanted to have a look at your records, see if someone I was looking for got picked up.'

Hammond gestures towards the screen next to Henry.

'All the recent cases are on that screen. Should be there.'

'Much obliged,' says Special Branch. 'This screen here, you say?'

Hammond waves him over, turning his back again.

NATIONALITY stares back at Henry.

He types in POL, the three-letter code for Poland. All he can think of.

He flashes a look at the records screen. Another case has been entered. He's at the bottom now.

OFFICER DEALING flashes up. Henry decides to use Dave Niblo's name. Last bit . . .

N . . . I . . . B . . .

Henry takes his eye off the keyboard for a second as he types in the last two letters, then RETURN.

Special Branch is at the screen now, peering at it, looking down the list.

The computer bleeps.

NAME NOT RECOGNISED, it informs.

Shit! He's hit 'K' instead of the 'L'. Who the fuck is Nibko?

Special Branch takes a step back from the screen, a pained look on his face, and reaches up to his breast pocket.

'Can't read that without my glasses. Too bloody small.'

Henry hits BACKSPACE, BACKSPACE . . .

Special Branch dons his specs and leans forward again.

'Let's have a look . . .'

L . . . O . . .

RETURN.

The list ripples downwards. Xiao and Henry disappear. Henry holds his breath . . .

'No,' says Special Branch. 'Doesn't seem to be here.'

Henry exhales, but something is drawing the copper's attention.

'Ali Baba,' he mutters. 'Funny name for a Pole.'

Henry moves forward and slides the letter from the doctor in front of Hammond.

'What's that?'

'It's a complaint.'

'Who from?'

'Returning resident.'

'A complaint regarding what?'

'Dunno. The usual.'

Hammond picks it up and looks at it. Then he crumples it in his hand and throws it in the bin.

'Too busy for interference like that,' he says. 'We're all too busy.'

Henry looks down at the paper ball nestling in the waste-paper basket.

'What are you doing?' Hammond asks, scanning his clipboard.

Henry, fatally, hesitates.

'Right. You can go and do British desk.'

Henry groans. 'Aaaaah, no.'

'Is something the matter?'

Henry doesn't reply, but knows the drop in his shoulders is visible. He turns and descends from the watchhouse.

'Bastard,' he mutters.

After the initial burst of relief at hiding the evidence of his connection with Xiao, he's starting to get worried again. Although it's not up there as a recent case, it's still on the system and his name's still there next to it. Whatever Thorough's working on, it's not standard procedure. The temptation is to keep quiet, ride it out, hope nobody picks it up and let the whole thing fade away. But that means spending the next week, month, God knows how long waiting for a tap on the shoulder, never really being sure it isn't going to come. He decides that when Thorough reappears, he'll have a word, get his mind put at ease. Only problem is, approaching Ed means stirring up something he might not want stirred up . . .

Rock and a hard place.

Four o'clock and Henry is back in the fold, the inner repose of three weeks away ground down like a hamster's head in a mechanical vice.

There are many who slag off the job, but deep down Henry, in the true spirit of alienation, thinks he is the only one who really hates it, who really thinks that what goes on, the shit that the likes of Speerpoint are into or the behaviour of ill-educated pricks like Dick Foster, is the pits. The truth is, Henry thinks it's beneath him. Starved of light in the dark arrivals hall, he fantasises about escape, his mind thrashes with agony and he becomes hateful. Which is just like they want him to be.

Not that it's difficult to be hateful. At Terminal C, where people are segregated by nationality *only*, you're in the real world; it spins by you every day and you understand what really makes it go round.

Arabs hate Jews. Everybody knows that. But at the same time you have to remember that the Mad Mullahs hate everybody else in the Middle East. What all the Gulf Arabs do agree about is their utter hatred for Palestinians first and North African Arabs second, the latter contempt shared by *all* Southern Europeans.

North Africans all hate blacks.

Eastern Europeans all hate blacks.

All Orientals hate blacks, make no bones about it, hold their noses if one comes near.

Black Americans hate black Caribbeans, who hate black Africans.

Black Africans from the south despise West Africans, who loathe East Africans.

Everybody hates Gippoes.

The Japanese hate the Koreans, think they're no better than the Chinese, who hate them back just as much. That said, they all detest the population of the Indian subcontinent who, when they're not at each others' throats, find the time to hate anyone with a black skin, especially Tamils.

Albanians hate Serbs, who hate Turks, who hate Russians, who hate Croats, who hate Greeks, who hate Macedonians, who hate Albanians.

Norwegians hate Swedes. Really.

Belgians hate each other.

People from Portsmouth *hate* people from Southampton.

In the real world, hatred is the only thing we *do* have in common.

And the Immigration Service runs on it. It is character-building when it comes to this kind of work; it is positively encouraged. It is a natural resource, available in abundance and self-generating. It grows exponentially. Every time Hammond or Bob the Bitch walk past in the corridor, you can feel it. They fucking hate you and you have no choice but to return the favour. Hatred breeds hatred, feeds off itself until the point where it engulfs you the second you walk through the door and you begin to carry it home with you. The art of the others is to take that hatred and focus it and redistribute it on the arriving passengers. Speerpoint has enough of it to refuse four hundred people a year and his reward is Daniella in bed every night. Still, she's just another fucking IO and Henry hates her too. Henry's hate, however, is dysfunctional. It is he, who sits there and says nothing and does nothing and doesn't have the guts to get up and walk out, who deserves the greatest contempt, and who gets it.

And whose shift has five hours to run.

Besides which, he's standing at the European Union desk, which means mainly Brits, untouchable for their repellence. Nobody else comes close.

Can anyone, *anyone*, really think their passport photograph is that funny?

The British.

Global village idiots.

Slags with big hair and fat thighs, mouths full of poison.

Short-haired tattooed freaks, telling you to keep the Pakis out.

Inadequates who think they're hot shit because they've come from New York.

'Experienced travellers', in a desperate hurry, probably for the toilets and a quick hand shandy.

Drunks telling you to let the Pakis in.

Best of all, thick old perverts who work in the Far East and bring their teenage Thai wives with them.

'I'm sorry,' says Henry to the clap-free baby doll. 'You can't come through this queue. This is for Europeans only.'

The queue comes to a stop. Restlessness courses down from the back.

'She's with me,' says a clapped-out old fart with a cancer tan and a strawberry nose. 'She's coming through here.'

'I can't deal with her here. I don't have the right stamps.'

Old Fart's face goes red, he steps forward, betrays his navvy's sensibility. 'She's not standing in a queue. I have rights.'

'It's procedure. If she's arriving with you for the first time, she has to see an Immigration Officer. I'm only here for Europeans.'

Baby Doll is clinging to hubby. 'Cung ong, Tommy, we go to orrer koo.'

Tommy relents. 'I'm sick of this persecution,' he shouts.

Someone in the queue sniggers.

Tommy loses it, lunges towards the laugh.

'You're just jealous,' he bawls. 'We love each other!'

'Give her one for me,' shouts a wag at the back.

Tommy and the love of his life fade away. The queue resumes with two slappers handing over their passports.

'Don't laugh at the photo,' one of them says.

Henry doesn't notice Ken McCartney creep up at his shoulder.

Ken is an institution at Terminal C and glories in the title of most senior IO. Any desire to be promoted during his thirty-eight years of service has been crushed out of him, replaced by an unnatural enthusiasm for the business of the Civil Service Caravanning Club.

Ken has, to be fair, seen it all, whether it was worth seeing or not. He was there when a Buddhist monk bit Jack Palmer in the ankle. He was there when Harry Dunlop, after one pint too many in the bar between flights, sicked up a pickled egg he'd eaten whole back over the French ambassador. He remembers the days when the airport was just one terminal and was the cushiest number in the service. Young whippersnappers like Ken were sent to the South Coast, this in the days when being an Immigration Officer would, he claims, be enough for complete strangers to buy you a pint and clap you on the back. Those days, as he never tires of telling anyone stupid enough to make eye contact, it was Frogs and Eye-ties you got to refuse, all coming to work as waiters. In those days, find a white shirt and a bow tie and *knock'emoffson.* They used to have a U-shaped ramp, so they could arrive and leave in one motion. Ken's darkest day came when we joined the Common Market, the day when Frogs and Eye-ties, not to mention your Dagoes, your Krauts, your Bubble and Squeaks, could walk into the country with a barrowful of bow ties and give him two fingers on the way. When European Community citizens became exempt from immigration control, a little piece of Ken died. Sure, he could have stayed down there among the busloads of

Polish Agricultural Volunteers and the ratbag duty-free smugglers, but he was so desperate to knock somebody, *anybody* off that he requested a transfer to the airport, where he could take his pick from the foreigner selection box.

Ken is also a Scot, a member of the Jock Squad, one of the disproportionate number the Immigration Service can claim as its own. In many ways, Henry would admit, they are temperamentally suited to the job. They relish its seamier side, and for many the ambition is to work after-entry, playing at Starsky & Hutch, kicking in doors and pulling Africans out of restaurant kitchens by the hair. The Jock Squad figures largely in the mythology of the service, the chosen few standing guard, railing against impossible odds, hard-working, hard-drinking, hard-refusing, hard-arteried hard cases. For them, immigration is a dream come true, the chance to act out a fantasy and dispense justice in a world of scrotes, toms and duffers they have created in their own minds.

So there's Ken, come to assist in forgery detection.

Immediately, Ken starts to talk. Henry keeps his eyes fixed on the queue of Brits and pseudo-Brits but Ken keeps talking as if pumped full of cocaine, which in a way he is. Terminal C is his drug, and the ravages of its abuse are apparent in his verbal diarrhoea.

'. . . Air Canada this is excuse me madam is this Air Canada from Toronto yes I thought so we weren't sure but now I can see it on your duty-free bag YYZ you wouldn't think that was the airport identification code for Toronto would you I mean how do they get YYZ from Toronto there's not a Y or a Z in it mind you nice country Canada I've got a cousin who lives in Edmonton married a Canadian girl yeah Air Canada they're using Airbuses now hold about a hundred more passengers than the old Boeings those mind you that's just another hundred bloody duffers when the Nigerians get their hands on one . . .'

Two skinheads reach the desk, just back from the Greek islands with a new strain of VD to add to their collection.

Henry waves them through.

'Here,' says one. 'Keeping the Pakis out, are you?'

Ken says nothing, but taps the side of his nose and winks at them.

Sunday afternoon defies gravity in its pedestrian slide down the clock face.

The Sudan flight is the next to come down. Groups of tall people with blank, damaged expressions move unsurely through the hall, stopping at every turn in the Tensabarriers as if negotiating a minefield. A first wave of young Salvadors hits the control, all without passports, all PA. They are sat down immediately, told to wait for an unspecified period as nobody has a clue as to when they will get round to being dealt with.

The Sudan donates a fair amount of new work, as it always does on a Sunday. With it comes a corollary increase in the Little Englander distemper of his colleagues. At a number of desks, one-sided arguments are in progress.

' . . . Where is your passport? . . .'

' . . . I know you speak English . . .'

'Where is your ticket? . . .'

'Stop lying to me . . .'

' . . . Want your benefits? Want your council house? Is that it? . . .'

' . . . There's nothing here for you . . .'

' . . . Where is your fucking ticket? . . .'

But this is pretty savage amusement. Everyone knows they've ripped up their passports and tickets. This is common practice. It allows new arrivals effectively to reinvent themselves. The name you give is the name you become and the nationality of your choosing simply has to be accepted. It is common for a country in the midst of civil war to be the source of a natural upsurge in refugees, not all of whom would be genuine. People from neighbouring countries can, on arriving without a passport, claim to be from there and reap the benefits of any Home Office amnesty on humanitarian grounds: Pakistanis posing as Afghans, Kenyans posing as Somalis, Albanians and Serbs pretending to be Kosovan. Occasionally, a set of questions is issued to be put to anyone claiming to be Somali or Afghan or Kosovan, but even genuine refugees were unlikely to be able to name the seven principal rivers of the country. Henry doubts whether he could name the seven principal rivers of Britain, should it ever come to that. The whole process is futile anyway, for to prove that people are not of one nationality is not to prove which one they actually are. Without that information, with no country of origin to return them to, without a ticket, boarding card or any proof of passage, there is no way of knowing where they have come from or who brought them.

They are here for the long haul. And they know it. There is something axiomatic in the behaviour of Somali refugees, as if they're the ones giving the instructions. Henry, partly out of a sense of contrariness, refuses to join in the universal condemnation of PA claimants as council-house-nicking, benefit-scrounging, opportunist scrotes. He claims to appreciate the motivation of those who have come, even for reasons outside the Geneva Convention, to try to improve the quality of their lives, which is what it really boils down to. But today, on a late Sunday afternoon, in a dark, dry arrivals hall, crammed with bodies and the sweet and sour stench of Third World cosmetics, Henry just wishes he were somewhere else and the whole affair is something he could read about over tea and marmalade on a Sunday morning with affected concern and have forgotten about by the time he goes to the pub at lunchtime.

Take your tired, your huddled masses, and throw them in the sea.

Henry gets one to deal with. The name on the landing card says Maxamed Ali. He is tall, with tight, dark hair congregating in tufts behind his ears. His skin is brown, dusty around the eyes and cheeks. He's wearing a windcheater zipped up to the neck and a pair of grey corduroy trousers which flare gently and are about two inches too short, revealing once-white socks and thin-soled black brogues. With tassels.

The bloke might as well have the word 'refugee' emblazoned on his forehead, thinks Henry. But at least Maxamed will give him something to do, hopefully take his mind off Thorough and the gook, away from the nebulous disquiet that the whole business is continuing to give him.

Henry takes him up to sit in the holding area, the pen.

The pen is full. It is a dark place, with a perpetual air of impending trouble and its own unique odour of spilled coffee and sweaty feet. The carpet clings politely to Henry's rubber soles. Henry's colleagues, generally the younger ones, are entering and leaving with more regularity now, all clutching yellow files that signify refugee cases. Hey, it's Sunday, it's their special day.

In each corner, groups of brooding young men have congregated along ethnic lines. The Turks lean forward, edgy at not being allowed to smoke, watching the others with barely repressed hatred. They talk among themselves and laugh coldly, unlike the West Africans opposite, who remain largely silent, communicating with eyes and slow gestures. Many of them sit so far back on the worn chairs that they are almost lying down. A few bear the red eyes and marked clothing of more than one night in detention, quite possibly having remained in this room for as much as seventy-two hours. There is a group of three Tamils, sitting quietly, occasionally all shaking their heads in agreement at something. The set of single Somalis is the largest, sitting around in a tight semicircle. Somalis are in the box seat and know it, so they have a more relaxed air than most. Even so, they have a menace of their own, partly to do with the absurd clothes many of them wear, super-cheap imitations of the baggy jeans and T-shirts favoured by American urban youth. Infants who stray too close to these collections are shepherded away by anxious mothers. As it is Sunday, there is no shortage of children in the pen. Younger ones will make a pretence of playing for a while when they first enter, but it is not long before they join their elders in the grip of a frantic boredom that can spill over into a fight or a half-hearted suicide attempt at any time. Dave Niblo's impostor has collapsed and is fast asleep. Refusal Shoes is sitting upright, clutching his briefcase to his chest. He is still trying, still acting the businessman. Even if it's true, it will do him no good, not after Speerpoint's thumb has swung down against you. Elsewhere inside the pen, families, couples or individuals, tourists from the wrong place or with the wrong face, make room for themselves.

Looking around, nowhere does Henry see Xiao.

This is where he should be.

WARNING – VIOLENT, he sees every time he blinks.

Henry leaves. At the entrance, next to the door with the security code (for it is officially a secure holding area), sits Jaz, a large, hulking figure and employee of the private security company which has the contract to supervise and transport immigration detainees. He is a middle-aged Indian, perennially jovial, though God knows why.

Henry steps up. 'Jaz, I've just put my Somali in the pen.'

'Fine, fine.'

'Busy in there,' comments Henry.

'Busy enough.' He is sitting by a window where he can look

in on his charges. One of them, Rwandan or Congolese or something, sidles up and taps on the glass. Jaz slides the window back.

'What do you want?' he bellows.

The man puts his fingers to his mouth.

'You greedy bugger,' says Jaz. 'You want more cake?'

He throws an individual wrapped slice of Madeira cake through the window, one from a large catering box of them he has at his feet.

'You want some cake?' Jaz asks Henry.

Henry declines. The African is still at the window, wanting something else.

'What you want now?'

The African makes a drinking motion.

'Fucking greedy bugger,' says Jaz, opening a tin box and throwing through the window a token for the drinks machine.

'Here, give me one,' says Henry. He catches the token that Jaz throws him and taps the combination lock on the pen door, letting himself back in. He saunters out a few seconds later and grabs a packet of biscuits, which he starts munching.

'Here, Jaz,' he asks. 'Did . . . erm . . . did Ed Thorough bring anyone in this afternoon? Chinese bloke?'

Jaz makes a face. 'I dunno. Let me have a look at the record.'

He peruses the logbook of every passenger who's been in the pen that day.

'Nope. Ed hasn't brought any passengers through . . .'

Henry breathes out through his nose, his mouth turned down.

'You want me to ask him?' says Jaz.

'Fucking hell. Don't do that,' Henry replies, taking a sip of coffee.

He doesn't see his nemesis creep into the room behind him.

'BRINKS! What do you think—?'

He doesn't finish his sentence. In shock at the uproar, Henry jumps a foot in the air and loses control of his coffee, which flies out of his hand and back over his shoulder.

He turns around.

Hammond. Soaked in coffee. Dribbling down behind his glasses.

Ouch.

'You have been notified that drinking coffee intended for detainees is strictly forbidden. You have now added to your difficulties by deliberately throwing coffee—'

'It was an accident.'

'—by deliberately – I repeat, deliberately – throwing coffee over a superior officer, which is I.'

Silence. Henry sniffs.

'What do you have to say for yourself?'

'It was an accident. You gave me a shock.'

'This is impudence on the grossest of scales and displays a flagrant disregard for the ban on hot drinks from the machine for the use of detainees only. You have not heard the last of this. Rest assured on that point. Rest assured on that, if on nothing else.'

Henry pauses, expecting more. He knows that Hammond can go on for hours like this. But not this time.

'Now get back out to work.'

Henry walks past him on the way out, but not without a glance back to Jaz and a sly wink.

Now that he has a case, even one as unremarkable as a refugee Salvador Dali, Henry can ignore the arrivals hall and the fuming queues and go back to the office to do some preliminary work. He has to start a file on the case. Obviously this presents limited but genuine opportunity to skive. Time skived on a Sunday is doubly valuable.

Inside, things are quiet. Roger Thorne is still there, reading a booklet of holiday offers put out by the local union branch. One or two are scattered elsewhere, including Ronan, who's leaning back on his chair with one foot against the desk.

He sees Henry and tilts his head, calling him over.

'By the way, you are playing in the Allports, aren't you?'

Participating in the once-a-year football tournament between Immigration Officers from all over the country was a mistake that Henry made once, but once only. The competition is noted for the regularity with which Corinthian enthusiasm spills over into brutal, tribal violence. Most of the trouble is caused by teams coming down from the north, who see it as a golden opportunity to lay into a few southern ponces.

Henry shakes his head.

'Why not?' asks Ronan.

'Because I don't want to get chopped by a bunch of Jock nutters who think it's Bannockburn all over again.'

Ronan laughs.

'You know what your problem is? You just don't understand the Celtic personality. It's all just a bit of fun.'

'I'm sorry. I just don't think it's necessary to paint your face blue for a friendly football game. That's all. You want to end up in traction, be my guest.'

'English poof.'

'Oh, touché.'

Henry takes the momentary pause that follows to change the subject, hopefully not being too obvious.

'So, that gook that Special Branch were after?'

'Yeah?'

'Anyone pick him up?' Henry asks, with a sniff designed to suggest a position close to disinterest.

'Not as far as I know.'

'And . . . what was it you said? They got the name from Onions?'

Ronan nods. 'Fucking unreal, isn't it?'

'So . . .' Henry says, faking bafflement now. 'He's got the name in his diary . . . why?'

Ronan rolls his eyes.

'Why do you think? He was his next job. Simple.'

'But . . . he never turned up?'

'Doesn't look like it.'

At which point Ed Thorough comes out from his preferred retreat of the forgery room at the far end of the room, hands stuffed into the pockets of his leather jacket. He walks past, looking serious. Henry summons up his courage. Fortune favours the brave, he fools himself.

'Ed?' he says, trying to intimate a working friendship with his tone. 'Need to have a word.'

Ed stops and looks down, as if viewing a weed in the garden. Henry shuffles.

'Get on all right with that no visa?'

'What?' Ed sneers.

'About that no Julius,' explains Henry, widening his eyes to suggest the importance of the matter. 'Bloke with the tattoo on his hand.'

'Don't know what you're fucking talking about,' answers Ed, steely-eyed, keeping his hands hard in his pockets and walking off.

Henry tries not to look cowed.

'What was that all about?' Ronan wants to know.

Henry tries to play it down, but he's grappling once more with his own fear of the sky falling in.

'Nothing. Nothing important. It's just that this afternoon he's frigging desperate to get this no-visa case off me.'

Ronan nods, picks something off the end of his tongue with a fingertip and inspects it. 'I've had the same thing with him,' he says. 'I had this bloke, some kind of Russian banker, so he was. Before I know it, Thorough's there, taking it off me, with approval from upstairs, he says. After, I put the name through the intelligence computer. Turns out this guy's of interest to the secret services.'

'Right . . .'

'You put two and two together . . .'

'And?'

'He's the office spook, in'he?'

It is a common if unsubstantiated rumour that in every Immigration Office there is one MI5 plant, posted to keep tabs on his colleagues and report back. Henry has always doubted it, thinking that if there were such a mole he wouldn't be able to keep his mouth shut about it. But if it were Ed Thorough, Henry thinks, then perhaps . . . Maybe he's working on something now, needs to keep it hush-hush . . . that would explain why he didn't want the chiefies to know . . . If that is the case, Henry was pretty stupid to mention it in full earshot like that.

'Here,' he says to Ronan. 'The bloke with Onions' stamp, the one the police picked up, he was Chinese, you said?'

'Yeah. Some kind of gook.'

'Then maybe Thorough, if he's the spook, maybe he's investigating it from the inside. You think?'

Ronan nods thoughtfully.

'Could be . . . yeah. Easily.'

Yeah, Henry says to himself, that might explain it. Might explain it . . .

From the corridor, Daniella appears, her tall, inviting form framed in the doorway. She throws a hand through her long hair and enters, making eye contact with Henry.

'Is it true?' she demands.

'What? What?' asks Ronan.

She stands beside him and leans forward, her hair touching the desk a few inches from his hand. Henry gets a whiff of her perfume. She smells . . . soapy.

'I've just heard that you threw a cup of coffee over Hammond.'

Ronan lets his chair rock forward, grabs both sides and jumps to its edge. 'You threw a cup of coffee over Shitbucket?'

Henry is smirking now, revelling in Daniella's attention. 'There was a cup of coffee which . . . may have found itself on to the Shitbucket, yes.'

Daniella claps her hands.

Ronan whoops with pleasure. 'What happened?' he asks.

'Oh, he was pissing me off, you know, giving me some lip, so I just threw it over him. Told him it was an accident, of course.'

Daniella has moved in behind Henry and grabbed him by both shoulders. 'My hero,' she says, shaking him. The movement throws her long, soft hair forward so that a few strands fall across Henry's cheek. Henry puts on a brave face, but somehow all of this is making him feel more miserable.

Eight o'clock now. Things are deceptively quiet. All the refugees the day has coughed up thus far have been removed from the control, which makes the CIOs a lot happier. Most are in the pen, but those who already have relatives here, usually a significant proportion, have gone home with them under instructions to return at a later date, the backlog swelled further. Maxamed's been sent downstairs to wait for his cousin or brother or whatever to collect him, less than happy that he's been in the country three hours but still hasn't been given any money. A few later arrivals drift in and out of the Port Medical Inspector's. These will not be the last. Late flights notoriously carry the dispossessed, and there are usually at least a half-dozen who have been roaming the transit lounge like care-in-the-community cases for hours before being picked up by airport security on their trawl after the last flight arrival.

CIOs make use of the quiet time to change over, the night shift chiefies bringing their watchhouse colleagues tea and biscuits before taking over from them. They discuss each other's tragic burdens over dunked HobNobs.

This time of the evening makes for strange bedfellows in terms of nationalities passing through Terminal C's sausage factory of pointlessness. Coming through now are flights from Yemen and Estonia. Perhaps these two nations have, at some point in history, had a mutual peace treaty. That aside, the only thing that binds them together is the fact that they both smell of alcohol. How this is possible on a flight from Yemen, a country as dry as a tinderbox, Henry doesn't know. As usual, Yemeni Airways International spews out its usual mixture of insignificant diplomats and toothless old blokes who look like Yasser Arafat's father but sound like Tommy Trinder. They are all residents of the East End, given this right by a guilt-ridden colonial power. Henry particularly likes their habit of wearing porkpie hats over their red and white tea towels.

'Hello,' Henry says to one of them.

'Awright, my son,' replies Mr Al-Rattah.

'Good trip?' asks Henry.

'Bluddy awfor'. I'm cream-crackered,' Mr Al-Rattah replies, looking around now. He sees his companion, a man three days older than God, hobbling into the arrivals hall. Mr Al-Rattah barks some Arabic at him, exhorting him to hurry up, to which he appends a perfunctory 'you old git.'

But Mr Al-Rattah's friend is not well. He is struggling for air, stopping every few steps, waving at his companion to wait up. His progress to the desks and beyond is agonising.

The lines move forward as the first few passengers from each spread themselves across the desks. Henry gets a painfully thin Estonian girl. She is wearing bleached jeans and a buttoned-up denim jacket. She hands Henry a green passport, clearly very new. Despite her anorexic appearance, Henry decides she has nice eyes and is disposed to land her.

Henry senses his body space being invaded from behind. An

arm suddenly appears over his shoulder and grabs the document.

He makes a three-quarter turn in his chair to see Chief Immigration Officer Rex Gibbons, who often does this kind of thing, staring avidly at the details page. Gibbons is short, squat and now only a few days from retirement. He has a twitch, one which contorts the left side of his face and produces a frog-like noise. He is also the man responsible for writing Henry's annual report. And it's that time of year again.

'Need to have a chat about your report some time,' he says.

'Right.'

'No need to be smug about it. I've got precious little good to say.'

'Cheers,' Henry mutters, before a nasty thought strikes him. As part of the reporting process, Gibbons will have to obtain a computer printout of all Henry's cases during the year. Each name will be listed. Including Xiao's . . .

Rex does night shifts quite regularly, as they leave him more time to tend to his wife, who has never been the same since being kidnapped and violated for two hours by the baboons at a safari park in Dorset. He is one of the number of CIOs who thinks that an IO's job is the best in the world and never really wanted promotion, so the curse is doubly cruel. As a result, he meddles, particularly in cases of young women, who, for some reason, he all suspects of being toms, of being on the game. 'How long is she coming for?' he asks Henry with a twitch and a snort.

'I don't know,' says Henry. 'I haven't asked her anything yet.'

'No need,' offers Rex. 'She's a tom, isn't she?'

The use of the word 'tom' to describe a prostitute is service-wide, and Henry supposes there is some merit in preserving these arcane expressions. Unfortunately, when Rex, with his West Country accent, uses the word, you're more likely to think of a 'tom' as being something grown on an allotment than someone who makes a living on their back.

'Definite tom,' he asserts. 'Does she speak any English?' he asks Henry.

'I don't know,' says Henry. 'I haven't asked her anything yet.'

Rex takes a step forward, snorts, grunts.

'Do you speak English?' he asks.

The girl screws up her face in a mixture of apology and embarrassment.

'Are you on the game?' A twitch sends his left arm flying away from his body.

The girl smiles innocently.

'She is,' says Rex, slowly looking her up and down. 'Just look at her. Probably enjoys it, n'all.'

He is prevented from going further by Guldeep, who approaches with another green passport from further up the row of desks. He waves it at Rex.

'This one's a friend of yours,' he says. 'Says they're coming here to study English.'

Rex sniffs and cocks his head. 'What d'you reckon?' he asks Guldeep.

'I think they are both on the fucking game. Couple of bloody toms, man.'

Rex rolls his tongue around his lips, his head snapping back with a twitch. 'Yeah, that's what I reckon. Maybe they turn tricks together, you know, like put on a show. I reckon there's blokes like to see that, you know, two girls *performing* together, kissing, touching each other, that sort of thing. Get some blokes off, that would. Tell you what, Guldeep, why don't I come and have a chat with yours. We'll take these ones over,' says Rex to Henry, who is relieved to have got rid. He points the girl in the direction of her friend, so they can be slobbered over by Rex then refused by Guldeep in what remains of his shift.

As is quite usual, a few of the lags make appearances late on. Roger Thorne, yawning extravagantly, comes out on to the control, not to do any work but just out of curiosity, to see if there's anyone to have a chat to.

He spots Fatima standing at the bottom of the stairs that lead to the watchhouse. Fatima is in her forties, plump and jolly, with a natural brownness to her skin tone. Henry thinks she may be from the Lebanon, but he isn't sure. She's chewing on a Mars bar, not fitting into her uniform too well these days. Fatima is the local representative for Saharan International Airways, who brought in today's flight from the Sudan. As such, she is a regular caller on Sunday evenings. Roger approaches and greets her with a hug and kisses on both cheeks.

'Ooh, Roger, you look the younger for every time I see you,' she says.

Roger makes a play of putting his hand in his pocket. 'How much do I owe you for saying such lovely things?' he laughs, bending at the knees and planting a light hand on her shoulder.

'You don't owe me nothing, Roger darling. I just like to bring a little cheer to all people round me. Costs nothing to bring a little cheer, you know.'

'Busy?' he asks.

'Rushing off my feet.'

By now, the full inheritance of her flight is known.

Twelve Somali PAs.

Ten Kenyan PAs.

Six Tanzanian PAs.

Three Nigerian PAs.

One Tamil PA(?).

Under one arm, she is carrying a bundle of about twenty yellow folders. Henry recognises these as Carriers Liability Files. Under the Act as amended in 1986, an airline bringing in any undocumented passenger is liable to a £2,000 fine.

Henry's arithmetic tells him that this one planeload has, in theory, cost the airline about £70,000. Fatima, as she collects more yellow files off passing IOs, always with a cheery smile and a word, doesn't seem too perturbed. They've never paid in the past and there's no likelihood they're going to start paying now.

'Heeellooo Henry,' she says as he heads back to the office.

'Fatima,' he replies.

'You found a nice girl yet?'

Henry smiles but doesn't answer.

'All these lovely girls working at the airport and you can't find one?'

'I don't really like the airport. I wouldn't want that to be what I had in common with someone.'

'You kidding? I love working here. It's so . . . cosmopolitan. Maybe you're not so cosmopolitan like me, thank you, love,' she says, stuffing two more passing files under her arm. 'The airport is like you travel the world but you no go nowhere.'

'Yeah,' says Henry. 'Terrific.'

Back in the office there is activity. Philip Heffer, cropped hair, in yellow shirt and one of the black, a-touch-too-small, Italian-made suits he always wears, is holding court. He has just returned from the Customs hall, where he has overseen the baggage search of a young, single, Brazilian male.

'I had him pegged for a sister the second I clapped eyes on him,' says Philip. 'Fluttering his eyelids at me, the little tart. He's probably just giving it away. And then . . . these.'

He points to several glossy magazines in a pile on the desk.

They are swooped on, colleagues poring over them with an educational fervour. Henry looks over someone's shoulder at a picture of a very fit but cross-eyed young man pissing into the face of another.

'I mean, what's wrong with holding hands?' asks Philip.

'What are you doing with him?' someone asks.

'Oh, he's a knock-off. He's on the game.'

'He coughed to that?'

'He's admitted to having worked here as a hairdresser, the bright-eyed little rat. It amounts to the same thing. I'm going to do him for working in breach and non-conducive.'

Non-conducive to the public good, as per Paragraph 320 of the immigration rules. The catch-all, just in case you don't like a face but haven't got a concrete reason to refuse it.

A moral judgement, but no surprise. Among Terminal C's most ruthless head-hunters there are a fair number of homosexuals, especially vigilant when it comes to those of their own persuasion.

Ed Thorough re-enters from the corridor and heads towards the forgery room, not without stopping to pick up one of the mags and flick through it, blinking slowly.

'See something you like, Mr Thorough?' asks Philip suggestively. 'Or are you just curious?'

The flash of lightning in Thorough's eye as he closes the magazine and faces Heffer is enough to silence everyone in the room.

'What did you say?'

Philip's face has gone bright red but he tries to stand his ground.

'Oh, fuck. If you can't take a joke . . .'

Thorough drops the magazine on to the desk.

'You're the fucking joke, you little worm. You and your fucking friends had just better watch where you tread.'

Philip starts to collect the Brazilian's effects.

'Ooh,' he retaliates. 'You can be just *too* butch, honey. You're giving me a hot flush with all your talk . . .'

Thorough sets his jaw at this, but Henry realises that he's too clever to be lured down Philip's conversational back alley, where he can't win. He gives Heffer, then Henry, a contemptuous look, a reminder to himself of something and he retreats into his personal chamber.

'There,' whispers Philip as the door closes. 'I always knew he was gay.'

At five to nine, the F shift get the nod to leave. Henry locks his stamp away and gets his coat. He leaves through the giant black door and follows a few straggling passengers on the way out.

He takes the escalator down and goes through the baggage hall. As ever, giant collections of unclaimed boxes and cases line the walls between agents' offices, still being sniffed at by a brace of shaven-headed Customs men and an excitable dog. One or two of the dozen carousels continue to circulate, solitary bags disappearing and reappearing, tottering at each bend.

At the far end of the hall, near the exit, a small crowd has gathered. There is some consternation on faces as they look down towards the floor. A couple more Customs officers are bent on their haunches. 'Move back,' one of them shouts. The crowd shuffles back a few paces. Through the bodies, Henry sees the prone figure of the ancient Yemeni, on his back, one arm flung over his chest, mouth clamped open. He is quite obviously dead.

'He just fell over, clutching his chest,' someone says.

'A heart attack,' someone says.

One of the Customs officers has found a fluorescent yellow coat with HM CUSTOMS emblazoned on it. He puts it over the body and head. Only the grey legs of his trousers and his tasselled shoes poke out.

'Blimey,' mutters Mr Al-Rattah, looking down, shaking with shock. 'He's brown bread.'

Henry stops and looks on for a moment, brow furrowed. To die in the baggage hall at Terminal C. That's bad.

He walks through the blue channel and into the landside arrivals building. In front of most shops and offices the shutters have come down. He passes one or two small gatherings of airport people: provincial underachievers who think working at the bureau de change is the last word in glamour, or mutton-dressed-as-lamb witches, employed by airlines but not young enough to be hostesses, their calves bulbs of granite from a lifetime in high heels.

Christ! wonders Henry. Was I always so cynical?

He walks quickly out, keen to avoid the attention of the afternoon refugee families dotted around the waiting areas. For them, with nowhere else to go, settling into the unforgiving, rigid plastic seats riveted into the floor, an endless night fighting the cold awaits. They're left just overnight, then plucked up the next morning for processing but many quite simply disappear, never to be heard of again. The number of absconders from Terminal C alone can be counted in their thousands. While this statistic causes much wringing of hands, the truth is that 'abbos' are somebody else's problem, no longer adding to the backlog of work.

Henry tiptoes down into the underground passage to the moving walkways that lead to the Tube. As usual, he proceeds as far along the platform as possible, where there is a small alcove, out of sight. There have been a spate of attacks on IOs down here recently, including one incident when a knife was pulled by a disgruntled Jamaican upset that his 'penpal' was the subject of an exclusion order.

Soon, the train grinds alongside. Henry gets up and boards an empty carriage.

Not too bad for a Sunday, he thinks, trying to kid himself.

In truth, he can't get that **WARNING – VIOLENT** stare out of his mind.

*

It's after half-ten by the time he gets back to the flat. Letting himself in, he kicks through the slithering hillock of junk mail collected on the doormat in the last month. Chocolate, his cat, is there to meet him, bitching for food, as usual. Twisting herself around his legs, she follows Henry into the kitchen.

Persuaded that it was a sound idea to own rather than rent, he bought the flat about six years ago, using what was left of his grandmother's money and the promise of a regular income from the immigration job. That was when he was still with Helen, the girlfriend he had had since university, the one he would have married . . . eventually.

Less than a year later she was gone, saying that it was all her, that it had nothing to do with him, that it was her who'd changed. And he let her go, Helen, with the long neck and the cobalt eyes . . .

It was only months later that he realised, as if struck by a flash of genius, that she left because nine months of living with a virtual zombie who either got in from work at eleven or got up for work at four in the morning was pissing her off. But zombies are notoriously slow to admit their faults. And anyway, by that time he had a nice dose of negative equity and he had to keep up the repayments and he owed the bank anyway and he couldn't just pack it in . . .

So now he shares the flat with Jerome, giving up what he pompously used to call his study to rent it out as a second bedroom. But Jerome's OK, mainly because he's never there, working as long-haul cabin crew. They see each other about once a month, when Jerome shares the gory details of a gay intercontinental love-life over a takeaway and nicked airline miniatures.

No Jerome tonight.

As Chocolate chomps on her half-tin of cordon bleu fish heads, Henry grabs a beer from the fridge and douses a large bowl of cornflakes with sugar and milk, carrying it through to the sitting room. In a cabinet under the telly, he keeps his collection of Westerns, about a hundred and twenty now, and struggles to select one. For some reason he wants John Wayne. Only the Duke will do tonight. But not a John Ford, nothing too ponderous, nothing too solemn.

He pulls one out.

Rio Bravo? For the hundredth time?

Comfort viewing.

He puts it in the machine.

When it gets to the part where Ward Bond finds out that the Duke's holding Joe Burdett in the jailhouse for murder and intends to keep him locked in there with Burdett's men swamping the town and that the Duke's got only Walter Brennan and Dean Martin for support, Henry picks up the remote.

'*A game-legged old man and a drunk*,' says Ward Bond. '*That's all you got?*'

Henry presses PAUSE.

'That's *what* I got,' he says.

PLAY

'*That's* what *I got*,' John Wayne echoes Henry.

REW

'*That's all you got?*'

'That's *what* I got,' Henry and Duke say together, making Henry smile. He used to tell people he wanted to direct a Western, but he knows that was just a displacement.

The truth is, he's always wanted to be *in* one.

Xiao stands in a shop doorway, bathed in darkness, waiting for his moment. He likes the way it was easy to disappear around here, that it seems to be a giant connection of hiding places, built to give people like him the advantage. No coincidence that the first Chinese here had chosen this place to make their homes.

The door he's watched for the last two hours opens slowly.

From the basement, bleary-eyed men appear at the top of the stairs, a minute or so between each one.

The card game is finished for the night.

Luck is on Xiao's side. The one he wants is last to come out, as the door closes and locks behind him. He counts some notes out before putting them into his pocket and – lucky again – crosses the road, right towards where Xiao lurks.

Xiao takes one step, putting himself in the perfect position. As the man walks by the door, only a foot away, Xiao moves on him from behind. Like lightning, he has slipped an arm around the man's neck, forcing his head up and back. His right leg swings forward and round. Sweeping it back quickly, he takes the man's foot off the ground, making escape impossible.

The knife is in his hand. He moves it up, in front of the man's face, flicks out the blade, waves it gently, allowing the faint sodium light of Chinatown to show it off. The man struggles for an instant, his star-tattooed hand reaches out, but Xiao pulls him closer and tighter before ramming the blade, point first, into his throat, twisting it hard, giving one tug, then a second as it pierces the windpipe with an apologetic hiss.

Xiao steps back, releases his embrace, but still holding the man's collar lets him spin out like in a dance move, so they are face to face. Even with life seeping quickly down his shirt front, there is time for recognition. And in the recognition, Xiao is pleased to see the surprise in his eye. It confirms what he suspected as to how the police had almost intercepted him, how his name had ended up in a dead man's diary and who'd put it there. And there it was, confession written in his eyes. Xiao had to kill him in order to know for sure. And now he knows he was right.

He lets the corpse drop.

chapter 2

strange dance

Monday – Casework Shift

'OK,' says Henry. 'Tell me why you need asylum in Britain.'

The interview room consists of a series of ten glass booths, from each of which every other is visible. It is packed with bodies, most of them in some kind of motion, radiating heat. An African woman is being questioned in one, surrounded by shifting infants, the youngest clamped to her bared breast. She responds to questions not with words but with movements of her eyelids and the elegant cocking of her chin. Others around her are more animated, stretching, getting up to remove jackets or sweaters in the increasing warmth. Interviewees range in their physical bearing from defiant denial to resigned indifference, or else rocking forward deliberately, sizing up their next move, perhaps considering the best moment to play their joker. Legal representatives sit, observing interviews with their clients, giving the illusion of industry on their behalf, making notes, stifling yawns, watching the clock to see matters don't fall outside their legal aid time-frame, God forbid.

The temperature compounds Henry's lethargy, but at least he is not alone.

Mr Thamootharampillai, Sri Lankan Tamil, sits opposite

him. He is here to explain why he is in fear of his life, but has the bearing of a man bored to tears, without the tears. The heat doesn't seem to be getting to him, however, as he sits, hunched forward, still wearing the dirty blue puffer jacket he arrived in this morning. Occasionally he looks across to his solicitor, Mr Penthandi of Penthandi & Associates, but Mr Penthandi is unable to assist, being soundly asleep. Mr Penthandi is a very correct man, small and slight of frame, dressed in a grey suit and the Fair Isle sweater he always wears. He is far too polite to snore.

Next to Henry sits Manny, the Tamil interpreter, palms down on the table. Manny is middle-aged, his wiry hair going grey. Manny has the contemptuous bearing of someone who has spent too long at Terminal C, but he is never rude to IOs. He knows which side his bread is buttered on.

Manny translates Henry's words in a flash. The interviewee shakes his head. This means yes. It's something you have to get used to.

He tells his story. His village near Jaffna has been targeted by the Sri Lankan authorities in their battle against the Tamil Tigers. Like most in his position, Mr Thamootharampillai makes one or two embellishments that don't quite ring true, trying to aggrandise his own status to give his claim more credibility. He claims to be on some committee of high command, actively involved in sabotage and disobedience. Sitting across the table, Henry finds it hard to imagine him disobeying a pedestrian signal.

'He's talking shit.' Manny offers his opinion, making sure Mr Penthandi is still asleep. 'He has a shop on the roadside.' Henry chooses to omit this from the interview record.

'Have you ever been detained?' asks Henry.

Manny translates.

Terry shakes his head.

'Yes,' says Manny.

'Can you tell me what happened?'

He tells what is, to Henry, a familiar story. The police burst into his family home, they drag him out of bed and begin a search of his property, looking for evidence of involvement with the Tigers. The soldiers plant Tiger leaflets in the house, and when they 'discover' them he is arrested. His wife screams and chases as they drag him away. She is struck with the butt of a rifle. He is taken to the police station, where he is thrown into a room with no windows and left for two days without food. On the third day, he is given some bread and then interrogated by more police. They are investigating a bomb attack in Colombo and have reason to believe that he knows the perpetrator. He is tied to a chair and struck repeatedly, then thrown to the ground and kicked. Other torture ensues: he is hung upside down and the soles of his feet are flayed; chilli powder is stuffed into his nose, making it impossible to breathe or to open his eyes. He is detained for a total of twelve days, during the course of which he is beaten at frequent and regular intervals. However, his health has deteriorated to such an extent that he is released. Following his return home and although still very ill, his brother persuades him that he should escape the country before the police decide he is well enough to be taken in and questioned further. He goes into hiding and his brother arranges tickets and passports through an unnamed agent, blah blah blah . . .

Henry has written it all down, betraying no response to this story. In truth, he feels nothing, having heard it, with minor variations, at least two hundred times and always via the verbal shorthand of a bored Home Office interpreter.

The Home Office insists that the process of interview in asylum cases is vital in assessing the credibility of claimants, but Henry has neither the information nor the will to try to trip anybody up over their stories. The cases exist only in a comfort zone of half-truth, impossible to contradict or verify, just as designed. Anyway, if you do meet a genuine refugee, a real shitting-bricks, Geneva Convention, running-for-his-life case, you know straight away. They're the ones who don't want to show you their scars, who find it virtually impossible to tell you their story coherently, who flinch at the memory of beatings and torture, who break down and can't get it all out. They do exist and you do meet them, despite what some say.

But Mr Thamootharampillai, if that is his real name (not the kind of name you'd make up), doesn't fit into that category. All that really counts is that he's here and will be here for beyond the foreseeable future. Nothing else matters.

As they move towards the end of the interview, Mr Penthandi begins to rouse himself, opening his eyes and then squeezing them tight shut a few times. He stretches and listens to the remainder, both hands wrapped around his chest, staring at the polystyrene tiles of the ceiling.

Before signing to confirm that the questionnaire is an accurate record of the interview, it has to be read back to the claimant. While Manny does this, Henry looks around.

Two booths away, tersely answering questions, is a Terminal C celebrity.

Samuel B (that's his given surname, one letter) is a West African of indeterminate nationality who claims to be Liberian but doesn't know the currency of Liberia or where it is on the map. His case, which has rumbled on for two years, finally exhausted the appeal process a few weeks ago. His solicitors have shrugged and told him that he would have to comply with removal to Accra, from where he originally came. For weeks, Samuel claimed ill health in the detention centre and even went on a hunger strike which lasted for three days. Ultimately, a Home Office doctor declared him fit to travel and escorts were hired to make sure he went all the way.

At first, it seemed that he would actually go, but Samuel waited until he was on the British Airways aircraft itself before putting his counter-measure into action. In the analysis that followed, Henry has to admit that what he did next was effective, with a simplicity in its conception that had made it almost beautiful.

Samuel deliberately shat himself.

He had followed this up with what was described as a 'strange dance' by witnesses, during which he had smeared excrement on the cabin windows and in his own hair. Of course, the captain had him booted off in a flash and the plane was delayed three hours while a team of fumigators made it airworthy once more.

Next to Samuel sits his new legal rep, a desiccated young girl with nasty acne around the mouth and a black polo neck sweater. She is one of the many trainees employed at a pittance by Miriam Cooper, undisputed *éminence grise* of obstructive solicitors. The young girl sombrely taking notes is one of a legion of sallow believers Miriam has at her disposal, all of them misguided enough to think it's a case of black against white. Just as the Home Office is out to discredit as many asylum seekers as possible, so Miriam Cooper Associates maintain that every one is a genuine refugee. Thus the trenches are dug and two equally absurd brands of moral indignation stand off. Henry doesn't envy them their position. Even he would probably prefer to stay on his side of the fence, where they at least pay you enough to get drunk. At least where he sits, you're allowed to let your frustration show to some extent. He wonders how they can bottle it up, how they can live with it, representing some of the knackers Miriam sends them out to, how they can keep faking it day in, day out . . .

Further down, Ronan is reading something out to an Asian man in his thirties. Henry recognises the piece of paper in Ronan's hands as an asylum refusal notice. The man looks as if he might be Indian, but asylum claims from India itself are fairly rare. Henry pegs him on probability as being an East

African Asian, almost certainly from Kenya. As Ronan reads to him in English, the man starts to shake in terror and grab at his own clothes. When Ronan reaches the end of the letter and tells him that he has to set directions for his removal back to Kenya, or wherever it is, the man sobs and gets out of his chair. Henry watches while Ronan tries to calm him down, but panic is eating him whole. Ronan's exhortations to calm are being drowned out by the man's agonised moans and the sound of him repeatedly banging his forehead off the desk in front of him. Banging. Hard.

The noise interrupts the readthrough of Henry's interview and every other going on. Ronan is forced to escort him out, clutching on to his shuddering shoulders. Order restored, the readthrough is completed. Manny hands the questionnaire back to Henry, who says there is just one more question to be asked.

'Is there anything you wish to add or amend to what you have said?'

Terry Tamil nods. He says something to Manny, who nods his understanding.

'He says that he knows that this is a country of fairness, where respect is given to human rights. He just wants to live in peace and hopes that one day his family will be able to join him. He is very grateful to the British state for allowing him to tell his story.'

Henry is a sucker for this kind of stuff.

He meets Ronan out in the casework office.

'That bloke all right?' asks Henry.

'He is now.'

'What did you do?'

Ronan drops his voice. 'I told him to appeal, phoned a lawyer for him.' If word of that got out, Ronan would have some explaining to do. Managers, the people who don't have to face potential violence in situations like those, would be baffled by such treacherousness. 'You know me,' Ronan adds with a grin. 'Path of least resistance. I'm not risking my neck for those fuckers,' he adds, gesturing towards the CIOs' office. 'I want to be in good health for my transfer to Sandgate.'

Henry smirks at such wishful thinking. To transfer to the sleepy coastal town of Sandgate-on-Sea, to *get Sandgate*, is the last word. Half the fucking service are after the quiet charms of Sandgate, two boats a day, six asylum cases a year, three pints before lunch.

Such competition breeds foul play.

In the normal run of things, transfers are dictated by seniority, but compassionate grounds are always given precedence. At this moment, there are some eighty compassionate applications for transfer to Sandgate, a port with a permanent staff of eleven. These range in theme from the ardours of long-distance travel to the need, on grounds of health, for proximity to the type of clay prevalent in the area.

The most common is the infirm spouse, mysteriously shepherded to Sandgate's burgeoning environs. Henry imagines there to be entire estates of infirm spouses, all sitting staring out of bungalow windows while the mail goes yellow and a doorstep full of milk turns sour. The infirm spouse is something of a speciality in the service, although long gone are the days when that alone would get you Sandgate. Nowadays your infirm spouse has to have been abducted and experimented on by aliens before you can get a look-in.

Ronan hasn't got a snowball in hell's chance.

'Are you on the list?'

Ronan coughs a laugh. 'Yeah, somewhere on page three. You?'

'Never bothered. What's the point?'

'You've got to be positive. Every time someone snuffs it, I'm one place further up. Maybe I'll get there while I still have a functioning prostate.' He looks around to see who's listening. 'As soon as Onions topped himself, everyone was on the phone to personnel, making sure that he got crossed off. Honestly.'

Henry rubs his brow, trying not to laugh. Ronan is whispering again, conspiratorial.

'Speaking of which, I've heard something *very* interesting.'

'Oh, yeah?'

'My brother's mate, the copper, he was in this morning to see the Bitch. I had a chat with him. Get this,' he says, really whispering now. 'They found another gook in Soho last night, murdered.'

Wide-eyed, Ronan draws a finger across his neck to signify means of death.

'Looks like a gang thing. But listen, on this corpse they find credit cards belonging to—'

Henry shrugs. 'Who?'

'Onions.'

After the uneasiness of last night had faded, Henry has let Onions, yesterday's business with the gook and Thorough flutter into the pending tray of his mind. But he doesn't like the uneasy feeling that being reminded of it is giving him.

'He *was* killed?'

Ronan shakes his head. 'That's the funny thing. They still think he killed himself. But now he's connected to another gook. And linked to a murder. My brother's mate told me that if Bob Gascoigne doesn't get to the bottom of it soon, the police aren't going to let it remain an internal matter. The Bitch has got a real aversion to having the rozzers sniffing around his patch.'

Henry slaps a hand to his forehead, then starts scratching it to explain away the involuntary action.

'So what's he going to do?'

'Well, if there was anybody else in on it with Onions, he'll have to find out who it is. And fast.'

Henry stands over the Xerox machine and begins to make photocopies of his interview notes. The copier, a real old bone-shaker, huffs and puffs, sighs and tuts as it churns out the copies.

Henry's brain is making a similar noise as he cranks it into gear.

He realises that there's a direct line of connection, via Onions' diary and the computer records, between himself and a gook lying in the mortuary with his throat cut. Somehow, he needs to break a link in the chain. Maybe if he can . . .

Tshutshutshubzzzzvmmmmmgrr

The copier wheezes to an unscheduled stop. Henry drops to his haunches, knees cracking, and opens the door to its mechanism. He sees the rogue piece of trapped paper and grabs it, pulling hard. It, of course, rips in half and Henry leans further in like a vet pulling something out of a cow's arse, his entire arm lost in the beast, forcing two fingers under some metal bar to try and release the paper that's left.

'Brinks!'

Henry looks up. It's Hammond.

'What are you doing?' he asks Henry.

'I'm . . . erm . . . trying to fix it. There's a—'

'Are you qualified as a photocopier repairman?'

'There's just a piece of pa—'

'Are you qualified to tamper with that machine, which is, I need not add, departmental property?'

'Hang on,' says Henry, feeling something start to give. 'Think I've got it . . .'

He pulls hard.

Something gives with a pop and flies out of the machine, past Henry.

When he looks up a moment later, Hammond stands above him, arms outstretched, looking down. Henry has dislodged the cartridge of photocopier toner with his exertions. It has hit the ground, opened somehow and covered Hammond in black soot from the chest down. He quivers, the skin under his chin actually quivers with rage.

'What have you done? What have you *done*?' screeches Hammond, his fists shaking around his ears.

Henry retracts his arm, bearing the ripped piece of paper.

'I'm sorry. It was—'

Hammond tries to wipe some of the muck off his shirt with the heel of his hand, but succeeds only in smudging it deeper into the man-made fibres.

'I'm reporting you for wilful damage to official equipment and for persistent and gross insubordination to superior grades.'

'It was an acc—'

'As it happens, I had come to inform you that the Port Commissioner wishes to see you. You, my lad, have some explaining to do.'

Oh, no! The gook yesterday. He knows. They've traced it back to him from the computer . . .

'Fine. I'll go and see him as soon as I've—'

'You will go immediately.'

'Sure. I just have to—'

'Now.'

'But—'

'That is an order.'

Henry looks up, still seated on the floor, legs stretched out.

'What, this is the army all of a sudden?'

Hammond takes a step forward so he can perform his little stamp, the sign that he is exasperated beyond the limits of corporeal tolerance. 'Yes,' he says. 'Yes. It is. It is the army. That's exactly what it is.'

Henry pushes himself off the floor and blinks slowly, once. He opens his mouth to say something, but Hammond stops him, standing on tiptoes and throwing out an arm to point in the direction of the Bitch's office. He wants to have the last word, but is so livid that he can only twist his mouth and growl like a stroke-sufferer.

'Gnaaarryowww,' he says.

Henry heads out and down the corridor, past the main office and the forgery room, past the staff toilets, past the tea room, past the Vale of Tears the chiefies call their office, past the training room and on, on, to the end of the line, to the last door, behind which lurks the Bitch himself, no doubt levering stones out of his cloven hooves with a Swiss army knife.

Panic manifests itself as a vice tightening in his gut. He rehearses responses. His fallback is easy – gave the case to Thorough to deal with and that was that. But it's a high-risk strategy. Leaving Ed to hang out to dry isn't an ideal solution to anything, but what choice does he have?

A few feet before the Bitch's office, on the left, is his secretary's room. Henry knocks on the open door and steps in.

She is typing, headphones stuck in ears, a macramé cardigan over her shoulders. Henry detects a whiff of gin.

'Hello, dear,' she says, sadly.

'I'm here to see the Commissioner.'

'Right, right. Well,' she says, brow furrowing, 'why don't you go in and wait for him. He should be back in a moment.'

'Right. Thanks.'

Henry enters the Bitch's office, half-expecting him to be in there anyway.

He is not.

The office itself is unique at Terminal C by having the benefit of real daylight. A wall of windows overlooks one of the runways, and planes can be seen landing almost silently through the reinforced glass, although Henry realises that it is not possible to see in from outside. The Bitch's desk faces away from the light, towards the door. It is uncluttered, no pictures of family, no mugs of tea. Both IN and OUT trays are empty. There is one man-sized pot plant in the corner. The only other decoration are a series of about a dozen black and white photographs hanging at eye level across the length of the interior wall. Henry takes a closer look.

Without ever having seen them before, he recognises what they are. Each shot is of the Terminal C arrivals hall, slightly different from now but not different enough to be mistaken. In each photo, the hall is full; not just full, Sunday-afternoon-with-the-Japs-going-through full but absolutely chocka, a shag-pile carpet of subcontinental humanity.

These photos are from early October 1986, taken some time in the week preceding the imposition of the visa requirement on India, Pakistan and Bangladesh. In the two or three weeks before 15 October 1986, when the shutters came down on visa-free travel to the old country, demand to enter the UK went ballistic. Airlines from those countries were laying on dozens of charters a day, cramming Terminal C to well beyond capacity with tens of thousands of visitors who must have thought they would never get a Julius. The queues stretched back to the gates where planes were arriving, and beyond. People were taking more than a day to get from their seat on the aircraft to the immigration desk, and nobody was losing their place in the queue, not even if it meant pissing or defecating right there where they stood.

The pressure was so intense that instructions came down to ask three questions: how long, what for, and who is your sponsor? Whatever the answer, the vast majority were refused immediately and sent straight back, entire floors of airport hotels being hired as detention accommodation for those who had to stay overnight. It was a time when reputations were forged among IOs, when you could ascend from sprog to lag in the space of one short day. Not that anyone was working short days. The overtime earned during that time paid for many a new car, holiday and conservatory extension. They still talk about it, the veterans of '86, eyes glazing over, heads shaking at the memory . . .

Henry's eye is caught by something else. There, behind the pot plant, he sees a video camera and tripod. Long-dormant professional interest draws him in. He is impressed. It's state of the art. He takes a look through the viewfinder and deftly gives the playback button a tap. He smiles at the silence of the Jap technology as the tape heads whir.

Outside, he hears voices. The Bitch is back, speaking tersely to his secretary.

'Who?' he hears him say.

The door opens and the Bitch enters, short, squat, pale complexion topped by light red hair clipped into a tonsure, rimless half-spectacles giving him the air of a Nazi eugenicist. He carries his shoulders curiously high, like a man who has been bolted together. Even with his size, his feet and hands seem disproportionally small to Henry. He carries a brown file under one arm.

'Mr Brinks,' he says. Henry notices the violence he performs on his vowels in trying to disguise his north-eastern accent. 'You'll sit.'

Henry takes a last look at the camera.

'Nice piece of equipment,' he comments.

'My office is being used for some filming,' explains the Bitch tersely. 'To improve interview techniques. Too many of our newer intake don't show enough aptitude when it comes to undermining passengers' credibility. You'll sit,' he says again, suggesting that the topic is closed.

Henry's chair, unlike the Bitch's, doesn't swivel.

'You know,' asks the Bitch, 'why you're here?'

Henry swallows, thinking: Fuck it. He knows.

'I . . . er . . .'

'You didn't expect it to be just overlooked, did you? You expect something as serious as this to be overlooked?'

Henry looks down at his lap, like a scolded schoolboy. The seriousness of the situation hits him like a bus.

'Well, what do you have to say?' the Bitch snaps.

'I . . . I had no control over what happened,' Henry stammers. 'It was taken away from me.'

'I don't see what mitigation you're claiming here. As you well know, you had no right to it in the first place.'

Henry looks up, quizzically. 'Eh?'

'That cup of coffee was the property of the department.'

The coffee he threw over Hammond. Henry gasps a laugh of relief.

'I'm not amused by this, Mr—' he checks the cover of the file before him 'Brinks.'

'I'm sorry,' says Henry, trying to turn down his smile. 'Accidents. It was an accident, both times.'

'Both times?'

'It was an accident. Yesterday.'

'A parapraxis, perhaps? The wish being father to the deed? The unconscious mind is a powerful tool. What was it that Shakespeare said? *The mind is a place that makes a heaven of hell and hell of heaven.* You ought not—'

'Sorry,' interrupts Henry, slightly pained. 'Sorry. It's Milton, actually.'

The Bitch stares.

'*Paradise Lost*,' explains Henry, looking away. 'I did a course on it. At college,' he adds apologetically. He remembers too late how much the Bitch likes to display his erudition. At least he doesn't tell him he's misquoted.

'Thank you for correcting me,' the Bitch growls. 'Milton,' he repeats.

The silence crushes Henry in the chest. 'Yeah. *Paradise Lo—*'

'Mr Brinks,' snaps the Bitch. 'I didn't go to college, unlike you. But I'm on this side of the desk and you're on that side, which must mean something.'

Henry shuts up but his eyes darken.

'Tell me,' the Bitch asks, brow creased quizzically. 'Are you new here?'

Henry recognises a classic Bitch tactic.

'Well, this is only my sixth year.'

'I don't recognise you.'

'I haven't been anywhere else.'

The Bitch opens the thin brown file, makes a concertina of his chin as he peers down at it. 'Yes, perhaps your anonymity is something to do with your failure to make a mark here. Your personnel file is hardly bulging with citations for work of a high standard.'

'That's my file?'

'No. You may not look at it,' says the Bitch, flipping it shut.

'I do what's asked of me,' says Henry, shuffling slightly. He decides to take a chance while his luck's in. 'Actually, yesterday I was assisting Ed Thorough in the Chinese exercise you asked him to undertake.'

'Chinese exercise?' asked the Bitch, voice clipped more than usual. Henry notices him straighten slightly in his chair. 'To what Chinese exercise are you referring?'

'The one you asked him to do.'

The Bitch's eyes wander for a moment and his brow furrows. Too late, Henry realises that any mention of gooks at this moment in time flies directly in the face of the cherished credo of *cover your back*.

Quite clearly, there was no fucking Chinese exercise.

Recovering himself, the Bitch sinks into his chair and allows a dramatic pause.

'Mr Brinks,' the Bitch goes on. 'What exactly is it that you *want* from life?'

The question throws Henry completely. He stifles a laugh.

'You want nothing?' asks the Bitch.

'No, no, it's just . . . It's a funny question.'

'So what is it that you want from life?' he repeats.

'What do I want from life?' Henry parrots, his mouth tightening. 'I suppose . . .'

But he doesn't suppose. Five years ago, he would have known. He could have rolled off a wish list as long as your arm. Five years ago, he had a future. Now the best he can hope for is just one decent night's sleep and to keep out of trouble . . .

Five years in this job and all that he really wants from life is to disappear . . . *They've done it. They've crushed the fucking life out of me. They've won . . .*

Henry can't answer. He sits, stunned by the realisation.

The Bitch sees that a reply is not coming. He displays no surprise, but sighs with an air that suggests his point of view has been affirmed.

'Do you know,' he says, 'that they call me the Bitch?'

Henry scratches his nose.

'No. I've never heard that.'

The Bitch smiles. 'You might think that I'm outraged. But I've come to think of it as a mark of respect. It pleases me.'

Henry nods. He follows a plane down with his eyes as it lands behind the Bitch.

'I have earned that respect,' the Bitch continues, 'not by doing solely what I was asked, but by taking responsibility, by taking charge. If you share the burden along with us, you become one of us. Forget what you were before fortune brought you here. Let *us* give you that something to live for. Embrace this career, Mr Brinks, embrace this career and the opportunities it offers. It's not a job that you're in here. It's a way of life. It's a way of life.'

Henry nods pensively. Tosser, he thinks.

'Or would you say you weren't suited to being an Immigration Officer?'

Henry feels flushed, somehow insulted. 'Not at all.'

'There's no shame in admitting you're not up to it. Not everyone has what it takes.'

He wants me to choke, is that it? thinks Henry. *He doesn't think I can do it. He doesn't think I'm up to doing a job as piss easy as this. Ignorant fat bastard. I wouldn't give him the satisfaction . . .*

'No problem. It's fine. I'm fine.'

The Bitch smiles and leans back, his chair creaking leather.

'Good. One of us, then. One of the family.'

Henry feels a shiver in his bowel.

'Go,' says the Bitch.

Someone has put a new toner cartridge in the photocopier, so Henry completes his task. As if to prove the Bitch's point, all he can think about is Onions' diary and the computer record connecting him to Xiao. Watching the sheets slide out, he knows that his encounter with the Bitch was a little too close for comfort. If he does get wind of the lost gook, never mind the rest of the business, he'll come down hard, make Henry another stuffed head in his trophy room of disciplinary order. It's up to Henry to make sure that can't happen. There is a way, but not one he can follow now, when the office is busy. Tomorrow, when he's on a night shift. That'll be the time . . .

He resolves to do it.

Back in the main office, big news has broken.

Big news.

One of the old lags at Sandgate has died.

Dead man's shoes.

Most attention is centred around a man in his fifties, his head a red cabbage atop a neck brace, the result of one of his numerous unassisted 'falls', as are the two crutches on either side of his chair, splayed outwards like oars. This is the legendary Jimmy Craddock, self-styled head-hunter with a heart and chirpy cockney geezer. Half-ten in the morning and he's already pissed. Or half-ten and he's never been sober. But Jimmy, by virtue of his prehistoric seniority, is top of the transfer list and, compassionate transfers aside, is in pole position for Sandgate.

'It was Derek Borthwicke,' explains Jimmy, barely able to control his excitement. 'You know Derek, used to work here. He had a stroke while he was sat in a car control booth. He fell halfway through the window and was waving his hand for help. All the cars thought he was waving them through. Apparently, it was the repeated blows to the head from passing wing mirrors that killed him. Shocker,' he adds with a boozy belch before tapping a nearby female colleague on the shoulder. 'I'm top of the list, you know. Top of the world . . .'

The news causes a flurry of activity as those on the waiting list dive for the telephones. Elsewhere, hushed conversations flourish among the old guard, each of them building up their own chances and undermining everybody else's.

Henry's attention is taken by Philip Heffer, who is looking for something, lifting up piles of paper, looking in any number of pigeonholes.

'Fuck,' he says. '*Oh, fuck.* Come on, darling, come to mother.'

Losing your stamp is no laughing matter. It is potentially a sacking offence. It leads to a conspiracy of silence between colleagues, once everyone has checked that theirs is safely in possession. Reporting it to a senior is a last resort, only after everything else has been exhausted and the inability to endorse passports is glaringly obvious. Philip is still some way from that point, but panic is beginning to set in, not least the creeping notion that it's nestling in the glove compartment of an X-reg Capri halfway back up the Great West Road.

'Oh, fuck,' says Philip. '*Fuckeroo.*'

He can't find it.

There but for the grace of God, thinks Henry.

Roger Thorne has just got off the phone and is keen to share his conversation.

'That was Raymond, one of the IOs at Sandgate. You remember him? His son went berserk with a paintball gun in an antiques fair, blinded two pensioners, had to have him put away in a special unit nearby?'

'Well?' asks Dave. 'What did he say?'

Roger shrugs. 'He said that the rest of the IOs there would like me to take Derek's place. I have a lot of old friends there.' He sniggers to himself. 'He was just reminding me of some of the scrapes we used to get into.'

'What's it got to do with the rest of the IOs?' asks Ronan, clearly irritated. 'I thought personnel made decisions on transfers.'

Roger chuckles.

'Come on, Ronan, you're a man of the world. You know there's a difference between how things are supposed to work and how they do work. It's not what you know . . .'

'Sounds bloody unfair to me,' says Ronan, peeved.

'Obviously it's tempting. But I told them no. I told them that it was Jimmy at the top of the list and if anyone deserved it, it was Jimmy. It's Jimmy's transfer,' he declares, as if it were his to give.

'You're a gent, Rodge,' announces Jimmy. 'Roger Thorne, a real gent.'

'Besides which,' continues Roger, 'can I really leave Terminal C? Would the place run as smoothly without me? Would it compromise the *operation* here? I'd hate to see relations with the airlines, with all the other agencies . . . I'd hate to think there was any strain here after I left . . . Not that I get any credit here. It's not as if my input is appreciated by senior management. See how they get on without me. Still, Sandgate . . . No, that's Jimmy's transfer, fair and square. Strictly between us, I'm getting offers from all quarters . . .' He raises a hand to stop an imaginary interruption. 'I can't say more than that.'

Meanwhile, Henry notices Dick Foster hunched over a telephone in the corner, listening in the main, but speaking very quietly when he has to. There is a sense of purpose in his watery eyes.

Henry sits in the windowless room, sucking in the air-conditioner's acid breath and understands what all the fuss is about.

Philip Heffer, meanwhile, is just happy to have his stamp back.

'It was down in the tea room,' he explains. 'I haven't been in there all day. Must have left it there from yesterday. I could have sworn I put it away. Anyway, got it back, thank Miss God.'

He turns the stamp upside down to inspect its underside. 'Funny,' he says. 'The date's wrong. What's it today?'

'The sixteenth,' someone tells him.

'Got the twenty-sixth here,' he explains, flipping it open to make the necessary adjustment. 'Funny . . .'

chapter 3

shoes in shoreditch

Tuesday/Wednesday – Night Shift

Henry drives down the motorway in his red E-reg Metro, pulled along in the slipstream of workers crawling back to the Home Counties. For Henry, the day's work is just beginning. Two days' work, in fact.

For him, night shifts are a necessary evil. Twelve consecutive hours in his own personal torture chamber are a daunting prospect, but two benefits mitigate. Those twelve hours represent two of the five days he has to work in a normal week. For the cost of one night away and a few hours' sleep the following morning, he has two days free. Not a bad trade-off. Equally, the office is considerably more sparsely populated. With only half a dozen colleagues present after ten o'clock, there is always plenty of opportunity to scuttle away to solitude in the huge office. Still, the prospect of work, of being there, of just crossing the threshold into the black hole makes his breathing heavy with sighs as he drives. He sees his own silhouette stretch and swing on the motorway signpost for the airport, lit by the headlights of the car behind. He feels, as he always does at this point on the road to work, a little bit like crying. But tonight, he has something personal to do, something that will sever his connection with the gook. Once and for all.

The office at night is revolting. The smell of the day's previous occupiers hangs heavy in the endlessly recycled air. Each room bears the wreckage of three shifts having come and two having left. Plastic cups everywhere, one or two having inevitably spilled their contents on to piles of forgotten papers, lazily cleared up. Newspapers rent asunder or dropped like dead sea birds everywhere. Clerical detritus: staplers, Tippex, Sellotape, hole punches, treasury tags, utterly ubiquitous. And bodies, lying around like more garbage, biorhythms at rock bottom, flung hard into chairs, feet up, heads back.

In the main office, Daniella is at the furthest table away. Next to her, their chairs pulled together, sits Speerpoint, sporting a new white-supremacist haircut. Henry's heart sinks as he realises that they're on nights together along with him. They both still have their coats on and are reading the same page of a newspaper. Speerpoint grasps the corner of the page.

'Finished?' he asks her.

She looks at him, smiles and nods.

He turns the page and, as they start reading again, allows his hand to drift upwards and stroke her gently on the cheek. She strains her neck slightly and rubs her face against his fingers as they caress her.

Henry feels sick at the prospect of a whole night of that. He opens his locker and gets his stamp, waiting for the Tannoy to pick him out and reel him in for some dirty job.

It takes two minutes.

'Henry Brinks to the watchhouse immediately. Hen-ry Burr-inks to the watch-house imm-ed-iat-e-ly. Please.'

The 'please' is ironically spat out. Henry rises, smiling weakly at the small chorus of 'oooh' from a group of colleagues, and trudges out. This time of day is usually quiet out on the control, a handful of Scandinavian businessmen drifting through with Olympian self-importance but little else. This is the time when cases from the afternoon are distributed, to be dealt with expeditiously before the onslaught of trouble that later flights inevitably bring.

Mad Sandy Reynolds in the watchhouse. Bloated Scottish CIO, known for gorging on cholesterol in the purest spirit of reckless self-endangerment. There he stands in the watchhouse, puffing and wheezing like a steam-powered clock, sweating chip fat and reeking of death. Popular legend has it that his arteries are so hard you could make a xylophone out of them. He is swigging from a mug of tea and eating a bacon sandwich. As the quintessential hard-drinking, hard-smoking, fat-sucking Caledonian, Sandy is a big wheel in the Jock Squad and is revered for the contempt in which he holds his own organs and his loathing of foreigners, particularly the English.

' . . . That's the fuckin' English all ower for ya,' he is saying to Jamie Vedhara, the only Asian CIO at Terminal C, known simply as the Token. Jamie's smiling, but uncomfortably. 'Prissing about with their fingers up each other's arseholes. That William Wallace, now, he had the right idea. Cut out their fucking hearts with a spoon and neck the bastards . . .'

This is all right for him to say. Anyone who tried to eat Sandy's heart is likely to break their teeth on it.

'What's that fucking economic migrant saying now?' This is Barry Venables, one of his colleagues, a Londoner, who enters the watchhouse, ready for a night duty. The curse struck Barry in the form of a milk float with a dodgy handbrake which rolled back down a hill into him. The result is a prosthetic leg, on which he pivots manfully. 'Economic migrant' is the name given to Sandy when at his most anglophobic. It is part of the brutal horseplay, but he doesn't like it.

'Aye, well, we'll soon have you meddling arse bandits out of our country and we'll be running our own show. Don't think we'll be giving out visas to arseholes like ye to come and piss on the Stone of Scone.'

'We'll be building the fuckin' wall again, mate. Who wants to go up there to see a load of porridge wogs rippin' their clothes off and getting back to nature. We'll have the fucking wall up again, keep your fuckin' AIDS plague and your crack-addicted teenage whores out of my country, mate.'

The Token slinks away. Sandy and Barry Venables on nights together means hours of this knockabout abuse. Sandy's presence also means one other thing: obligatory curry. Henry sighs at the thought. Sandy notices him.

'What the fuck do you want?'

'You put a call out for me.'

'Did I? Christ, we must be fuckin' desperate. There's two Russians for you to knock off. Just don't take too long with it. The ZX is coming in tonight.'

Bad news. ZX is the dreaded two-letter airline code for Air International of Nigeria.

This isn't a normal night for its arrival, not that it is coming at night. Half-past one in the morning. This is exactly the kind of thing that the Nigeria does. Very inconsiderate.

Air International of Nigeria means one thing. Work. The culture of Terminal C dictates this. Nigerian passengers cost the Home Office more man hours per capita than any other nationality, barring Libyans or Cubans whom you might see once every two years. This is mainly because, with Libyans and Cubans, nobody is ever sure what to do, and time drags on while a course of action is reached by committee. With Nigerians, on the other hand, everybody knows what to do.

Hold them up. Sit them down. Fine-tooth comb.

Nigerians enjoy mythic status at Terminal C, ingrained early into the neophyte. They figure in sketches at the office Christmas party every year; they populate untold anecdotes, apocryphal or otherwise; people new to the job spend hours trying to mimic their West African breathiness. Your first Nigerian flight is viewed as a kind of initiation, to be approached with fear while your senior colleagues breeze it.

According to perceived wisdom, Nigeria is a land of monsters, a country populated exclusively by congenital liars and habitual criminals. Even Henry, who kids himself that he's colour-blind and gives everyone a fair chance, has to concede that Nigerians produce a vast quantity of casework. No corner of immigration abuse is unknown to them. Forgeries, multiple identities, benefit fraud, bogus marriages, vexatious claims to asylum, Nigerians are strangers to none of it. And there's a gospel to prove it, the reams of computer statistics, the long-as-your-arm list of cases bearing the ubiquitous three-letter code NGA. Ronan, amateur philosopher and post-modern thinker on immigration matters, had once drunkenly said to Henry that despite the statistics, Nigerians didn't break the immigration rules any more than they were supposed to. Henry thought there might be something in this, although in truth he doesn't really think he had quite understood.

All of this is, however, of secondary importance. He is primarily pissed off to see it, not from any sense of indignation, but from another prevailing tendency.

Idleness.

'Is that right?' he asks, still staring at the screen. 'The ZX coming in. At half-one in the morning?'

Sandy grunts the affirmative, but very much in a way designed to let Henry know that it doesn't matter what time it comes in, it's his job to deal with it.

'Christ,' Henry tuts. 'That's kip out of the window.' Sleeping on a night shift is standard practice, assuming there are no flights. There are even folding beds hidden in a cupboard in the clerical office which can be wheeled out to various offices – but for old-timers like Sandy, it's something they don't like to be aired. He doesn't go for Henry's bait, but changes the subject.

'I thought you had two Russians to deal with.'

And that's that. Your mission, should you choose to accept it, not that there is a choice. Henry trudges down the stairs, consoling himself with the thought that if he drags it out long enough, he might miss the rest of tonight's flights. But not, of course, the ZX.

Fifteen minutes later he is back in the interview rooms, facing the wall in the glass booth furthest away from the entrance. Only one other booth is being used; an IO Henry doesn't know the name of is talking to a Somali, who is listening, elbows on the desk, chin resting on the palms of his hands.

In front of Henry is a file and two green passports, not Russian, as Sandy said, but Lithuanian, although the distinction would be lost on him. Opposite him are the two poor boys, fake leather jackets clinging apologetically to sloped shoulders, answering Henry's questions in passable English. He goes through the motions – how long had they been planning their trip? how much money for their trip? whose idea was the trip? first time abroad? why only single tickets? how long had they been saving for the trip? how much do you earn? etc. etc. Everyone realises tacitly that nothing they could say would make one iota of difference to the final outcome. He halts the interview for a few seconds to look over his notes. As it stands, everything against these two is circumstantial: the single ticket, the lack of money, their situation at home, the very place they came from. Most IOs would have been perfectly content to refuse on this basis alone, on the passengers' credibility.

Henry detests credibility cases.

Paragraph 43 of the immigration rules, as enforced under the Immigration Act (1971), dictates that, in order to gain Leave to Enter to the United Kingdom, it is necessary to satisfy an Immigration Officer that you qualify. But, as Henry knows, some are more easy to satisfy than others and parameters of satisfaction change on a day-to-day basis. God help the first backpacker coming for a week who meets Simon Topp across the desk the day after Millwall have been beaten. Staring across at them, Henry is quite prepared to believe that these two are good, God-fearing boys who haven't come to look for a job here because their lives are shit where they come from, who will stay for a few days and then leave. He knows it's not true, but he wants to believe it. He wants to let them go and to bask for a few seconds in the warmth of their gratitude.

But he cannot. He is expected to knock them off and bounce them. If he doesn't, he will be answerable to mad Sandy Reynolds and no amount of Baltic thanks is worth that.

It's just easier to refuse them. Especially tonight, when he has more important things to worry about . . .

'OK,' he says. 'I have to go and talk to my boss now.'

This is the part Henry hates the most.

Referring the case.

Any Immigration Officer has the right to land a passenger, but in order to refuse one it has to go through a CIO, even when, as in this case, he's already been told to knock these boys off. If you're a head-hunter, this procedure works to your advantage, because you can tell chiefy whatever you want to get your scrote bounced. And chiefy is, ninety-nine times out of a hundred, happy to oblige. For the old lag class, it's often sufficient to pop your head around the door and say 'he's a refusal' in order to get the nod. But if, as happens to Henry, you don't *always* want to refuse, it's an uphill struggle. More often than not, he loses out so that now he refers only the most open and shut cases, like this one.

Sandy's there, in the watchhouse, ramming a Mars bar into his gob.

'Where've you been?' he asks. 'What have you done with those Russkies?'

'Lithuanians. They're Lithuanians.'

'Who gives a flying fuck? Christ! Just two fucking Bolsheviks.'

'Right, well, I've interviewed them.'

The Mars bar gone, Sandy starts on a Twix. 'And?' he asks through a mouthful of chocolate-covered caramel.

'They want to work.'

'I bet they fucking do.'

Henry looks down at his notes. 'Single tickets, fifty quid each, no contacts here. I think they're pretty obviously refusals.'

Sandy swallows. 'Do you, now? I'll be the judge of that, son. What I don't need is you thinking. What I need is you getting out there and stamping fucking passports.'

'So you want me to land them?'

'Don't be fucking clever with me, ya wee shite. I want you to bounce the little red bastards and get a fucking move on about it.'

Henry looks down at the two files. 'You want me to give them temporary admission overnight?'

Sandy almost coughs out his Bounty bar. 'You are fucking kiddin'? You *are fucking kidding me*?'

'I just thought . . .'

'Jesus! Temporary admission? Where do they find you people? There must be some real fucking IOs out there.'

He swings his leg and sends a metal wastepaper basket flying out of the watchhouse door, clattering down the steps.

'DETAIN! DETAIN! DETAIN!'

Henry scuttles out.

'Oh, by the way,' says Sandy as Henry reaches the bottom of the steps. 'What curry will you be wanting?'

Henry sits down at the computer and enters his password. The screen stretches into life and offers him a menu of options. He selects option 6 – REFUSE LEAVE TO ENTER. He knows the button is number 6 because it lies between 5 and 7 – the number has been erased through use.

A few seconds later, the printer is churning out the bad news in the form of a refusal notice to be served on each of the two Lithuanians. The computer screen is flashing at Henry with a question. **DETAIN? (Y/N)**

When it comes to locking people up, the Immigration Act (1971) gives IOs and chiefies powers that would make your average South American generalissimo froth with envy. Basically, under the Act anyone served with form IS81 by Henry or any of his colleagues can be detained without charge for an indefinite period, for entirely arbitrary reasons which do not have to be disclosed outside the environs of the service. The initial decision to detain is taken by a chiefy, usually with the goading of a head-hunting IO. Leaving the decision to withdraw somebody's liberty to as maladjusted a group of power-crazed bigots as these may seem perverse, but then nobody bargained for the fact that to detain, to *bang up*, has become a totemistic practice among immigration personnel, priapic proof of dedication to the cause. To them, the thought of one empty immigration detention space is an abhorrent vacuum. If there is a space, it must be used, because it exists. As fast as more spaces are found, as more detention centres are built, they are filled. The spillover winds up in prison accommodation, some poor bastard spending months behind bars without charge because an amoebic life form down the food chain of public service decides on a guess or a whim that they would not comply with temporary admission.

The irony, which Henry knows to be true but will never see proved, is that if anyone banged those charlies up for a night, they'd be pissing themselves and shrieking for mummy before the bolt even clanked shut on the cell door.

But Henry, cowardly bastard that he is, presses Y and goes along with it.

The detention papers spill out of the printer, correctly worded to pass his two boys over to the tender mercies of the privatised security company that handles their incarceration for the night. Henry trudges off to tell them: a) they've been knocked off; b) they're being banged up; c) they'll be bounced tomorrow, first thing.

They don't take it too bad.

By the time he's finished, at least the last scheduled flight has gone through and the bar down in the arrivals area is still open.

Henry goes down, leans over the end of the bar to make himself seen and orders a pint of Guinness.

Those who are down there, half of the night shift, are taking turns to read an article in a newspaper. Dave Niblo, who's still there three hours after his shift finished, is looking at it now, shaking his head beerily.

'It's a shocker,' he comments, putting the folded paper down on the bar next to Henry. 'Onions mixed up with those toerags . . .'

Henry glances down. The article concerns a man found dead from a knife wound in Chinatown, presumably the one Ronan was on about, the one with Onions' credit cards in his pocket. There's no reference to that part of the story. If it was true, then they *were* covering it up, trying to protect the good name of the service . . .

Good name? The thought makes Henry smirk as he reads further.

. . . police are investigating the possibility of this being the work of Chinese organised criminals. The particular nature of the attack and the presence of a black, star-shaped tattoo on the back of the victim's hand, a known Triad marking . . .

The conversation goes on around him.

'I heard they're not sending anyone to his funeral . . .'

'Fair enough. He was up to something . . .'

'Wouldn't be the first . . .'

'Yeah, but you never know. Maybe they were threatening him.'

'Or blackmail.'

'Yeah. There was a bloke at Terminal B, got done for facilitating Turks, remember. Went down for three years. He wanted out, but they said they'd go after his kids. What choice has a bloke got?'

That's it, thinks Henry. Tonight is definitely the night.

'Here, Brinks,' shouts Speerpoint, twiddling with a knob on the walkie-talkie that obtrusively hangs from his trouser belt. 'I hear you've been endearing yourself to Hammond.'

Daniella is next to him, smoking a rare cigarette unconvincingly, rocking her head back to blow the smoke as far away as possible.

'Something like that,' mutters Henry.

'Might jeopardise your chances of promotion.'

Henry smiles weakly as he sips.

'Yeah, right,' he says. 'I'll leave the arsekissing to you.'

'Oooh,' laughs Speerpoint. 'Got me all wrong, mate. Who wants to be chiefy? Where's the fun in that? Who's Dex gunna race if I do that?'

Dex is Dexter Fraser-Gill, a repellent little shit in the Speerpoint mould who learned his xenophobia at a noted public school. Dex and Speerpoint are in a well-publicised competition to see who can rack up the most refusals in one calendar year. There's a pint riding on it.

'Who's ahead?' asks Dave Niblo.

'Dex is. Just. But the little git's cheating. He's been volunteering to do asylum refusals, doing six or seven a shift. It's not fair.'

Daniella pipes up. 'You said refusals. A refusal is a refusal.'

Speerpoint turns his lip. 'Yeah, but an asylum refusal? Come on. I mean, they get an appeal, don't they? Where's the fun in that? Where's the *skill* in that? Anyway, don't you worry, I'm not far behind. Had a few family groups recently. I'll break five hundred before he does.'

Five hundred? It's November. Henry doubts whether he's much into double figures.

'Anyway,' continues Speerpoint. 'I reckon my refusal stats are going to get me ECO this year.'

Entry Clearance Officer. A posting abroad, dishing out visas. A chance to make a shit-load of cash and be nasty to darkies *chez eux*. The majority of IOs want ECO. Most apply every year and get nowhere, but the likes of Speerpoint normally waltz into it. For his part, Henry doesn't see the appeal in living on a compound in the Third World, working on your alcohol dependency and being patronised by forty-something Foreign Office weirdos who feel happier paying for a woman than talking to one.

'You've applied?' Henry asks him.

'Yeah. Got a "highly suitable" report. Loo-king good.'

Henry glances at Daniella. 'So what are you going to do if he pisses off for three years?' he asks, as matter-of-factly as he can.

She looks down into her drink.

'She's coming with me,' says Speerpoint.

'I'll go with him,' says Daniella, tossing her hair back.

Married, thinks Henry. That means they're getting married.

'Right,' says Henry and takes a heavy swig of beer, some of which winds up down his front.

The walkie-talkie on Speerpoint's belt crackles.

'*. . . Kestrel Nest to Kestrel One. Kestrel Nest to Kestrel One. Are you receiving, Kestrel One*?' says a recognisable Scottish voice.

Speerpoint pulls the radio to his mouth. 'Roger that, Kestrel Nest. This is Kestrel One receiving. Go ahead, Sandy. Over.'

'*You'd better be getting your arses up here, Kestrel One. Over.*'

'Message understood, Kestrel Nest . . . Kestrel Nest, do we have a situation?'

'You're bloody right, Kestrel One. Your curries are getting cold.'

Back upstairs, Henry tucks into his biryani but starts to feel full after three forkfuls.

Sandy Reynolds sits, a pint glass half-full of red wine in hand, surrounded by the fruits of the Taj Mahal, directly in front of the television. There is football on, the highlights of an international friendly between England and Cameroon.

'Come on, you macaroons,' he says to the television, wrenching off a chunk of naan which he dips into a plastic cup of ghee specially supplied by the restaurant as a favour. 'Come on, the macaroons. Get into this English pish.'

A further call goes out over the Tannoy that the curry has arrived. Officers drift in and claim what is theirs. Daniella and Speerpoint pick up a chef's special meal for two and disappear to enjoy it tête-à-tête.

'Och!' screams Sandy Reynolds, jumping out of his chair and pushing back his specs with ghee-smothered fingers. 'Send that English cunt off! Dirty fucking bastard! Are you going to eat that?' he asks Henry, pointing at the remains of his biryani.

'Have it,' says Henry, pushing it across.

'Don't like to see waste,' says Sandy, pouring the remains of the clarified butter over Henry's dinner. 'What time's the Nigeria showing?' he asks Barry Venables.

'It's gone back another hour. Back to three o'clock.'

Assorted groans.

'Yes,' adds Venables, wiping a grubby fork down the polyester trousers he always wears and addressing a lamb bhuna, 'they'll all be sitting up there, working on their stories. *Aah, I have come to buy spare motor parts,*' he suggests in his impersonation (pretty good, Henry would admit) of a Nigerian passenger. This prompts one or two others to try out their *aahs* in preparation.

On the television, the camera has turned to a small but vocal group of Cameroon supporters among the crowd, a riot of flag-waving colour.

'Jesus Christ, do you see that?' says Mad Sandy. 'Did you let them fuckers in?' he asks Venables. 'They better not be giving out bloody visas to every fucking shoeshine who wants to watch a football match.'

'At least they don't invade the pitch and break the goals if they lose.'

'What did you fucking say?' says Sandy, animated but still staring at the screen. 'That's what we do when we *fucking beat* you English softarses . . .'

At a few minutes to midnight, Henry reckons it's safe to disappear. With the Nigeria coming in at around three, he has offered to volunteer to sit up from two o'clock to man the watchhouse. That's the time when he'll do what he has to do, when it's quiet . . .

That still gives him a couple of hours or so to have a lie down, maybe grab a little sleep.

He creeps into the office that he reserved earlier in the evening. There lies the small, metal-framed bed, his sleeping bag on top of the mattress. He strips down to T-shirt, boxers and socks and switches off the light before slipping into the bag. The mattress stinks of stale cigarettes and sweat. Henry wonders, as he always does, how many times Dick Foster has slept on this particular one and exactly what practices he chose to engage in.

He closes his eyes, but the air-conditioners scream at him to stay awake. He furrows his brow and begins to feel a headache whirl into being like a tornado just above his left eye socket.

The curry gurgles in his gut.

Through the paper-thin wall to the next office, he hears a sound, like a hissing, then a moan, as if someone's having a nightmare. Then the moaning, then the hiss. Except the moan and the hiss are simultaneous. Then the hiss stops altogether and there's the moan again, very quiet and then the noise stops. Then it starts again, after a few seconds, and another moan with it, but this one is shorter and sharper and . . . deeper, and then the first moan is a little louder and longer and rhythmic now and Henry realises that's it's Daniella . . .

Oh, no! Not in the next room! Not with Speerpoint in the next sodding room! Henry clutches a hand to his forehead. No way . . .

Henry knows instinctively that she's on top, straddling him, looking down, gently lifting and lowering her hips with him in her, brushing the hair out of her face, looking down at him, smiling.

And for some reason, that makes it worse.

Henry groans deliberately, hoping to make them stop, but it doesn't. Daniella comes first, followed by him a few seconds later, and he lies in the next room, icy-awake, taunted by Speerpoint's soft, satisfied snores.

At five to two, Henry gets up and dresses. On his way to the watchhouse, he pops into the tea room to get a coffee from the machine. The two chiefies are the only ones left. He finds them deep in plonk-sodden reminiscence – a litany of meaningless names, some celebrated for their alcoholism, some for their refusal statistics, some for their number of failed marriages inside the service, all of them moved on to other ports or other sections, to jobs in offices with new acronyms whose purpose is opaque.

They are talking about someone Henry has never heard of

called Dennis Bough, but who interests him because he is someone who achieved the *coup de grâce* of a transfer to Sandgate-on-Sea.

'. . . Oh, aye, he pulled it off,' Sandy is explaining, chewing on a Wagon Wheel. 'First of all, he bought a house down there and he was driving a 300-mile round trip every day. Then he started going to the doctor and complaining about his sciatica.'

'This is the doctor who happens to be his brother?'

'Oh, fuck, aye. He was no fool, Dennis. So he's dropping hints that he can't be driving these distances because of his sciatica, so personnel starts making noises about a medical retirement and only half a pension. Now he's shitting himself. So what he does is he moves his parents from Kirkcaldy down to Sandgate on doctor's advice.'

'Christ. How old were they?'

'That's the fucking point. Dennis is no spring fucking chicken. These two are both in their eighties. He makes them sell up, move six hundred miles south and he sticks them both in a home, gets a note from his brother, the doctor, that they both have fucking Alzheimer's and flings that one at personnel, claiming that he has to be there to look after them and has to keep working to support them. That's how he got his compassionate out of here.'

'What about Diane?'

Sandy shrugs. 'She didn't want to leave London. So he left her. Christ, we're talking about a transfer to Sandgate here. She doesn't want it, fuck her. Anyway, now she's engaged to some CIO at Terminal B whose last wife used to be at headquarters. She was the one who fell off the Mersey ferry and drowned last year.'

'You heard about Derek Borthwicke, then?'

'Oh, aye. Empty chair at Sandgate. There'll be some bloody scrap for that.'

'Jimmy's top of the list, isn't he?'

'Aye, but that doesn't count for much when the sob stories start.'

Venables nods. 'Still,' he says after a pause. 'Sandgate. Bloody quiet.'

'Oh, fuck, aye. Too bloody quiet for me.' Sandy pulls out a quarter-bottle of whisky from his jacket. 'Terminal C for me. Cut and thrust, that's what keeps me alive. Real immigration work, not pissing about with boozecruisers and wading in stowaway shite.'

'No, I agree,' says Venables, accepting a swig of the hard stuff.

'You can make it at C, you can make it anywhere,' says Sandy.

As Henry leaves again, sipping his coffee, a melancholy silence has fallen between them.

Time for action.

A couple of minutes past two, and Henry finds himself alone in the near darkness of the watchhouse. The air-conditioning never rests, making him cold and sucking the moisture out of his face and the ends of his fingers. For the moment, he is startled into wakefulness, but he knows that sleep will bounce back off the ropes and grapple with him again soon.

The hall is not entirely empty. Away in the far corner two Sikh men are working. One is sitting atop a high scaffold on wheels, attacking the polystyrene ceiling tiles with a large feather duster. His colleague is below pushing the scaffold as he dusts each particular section. They are in constant conversation. Henry does not understand their language, but he knows they are talking just for the sake of it, just to prevent silence from gaining a foothold between them at this desperate hour.

The unwanted curry hangs heavy in his gut, and the stench of beer lingers in his mouth and nostrils. The cold starts to bite further, and Henry dives back into the office to get his fleece, which he pulls on. The Sikh men see him and wave cheerily. Henry hates the bogus camaraderie of the airport but he waves back so as not to appear rude. He checks the small flight screen for the time of the Nigerian flight: 3.15, it says. Over an hour to get it done . . .

He grabs the Anglepoise light on the counter next to him and, holding it upside down, copies a series of four numbers that are on a piece of paper taped to the underside. Henry's not supposed to know these numbers, but Ronan told him where they were kept. It was never a piece of information he expected to have to use, but now he's grateful to whichever chiefy has the bad memory.

Quickly he's over to the opposite corner of the watchhouse, squatting down to address the lock on the small safe that's kept there. He follows the combination he's copied down. Five turns to the right . . . four to the left . . . He stops at every turn and stands up to look around.

All clear.

With the last, single turn to the right, the lock catches and Henry is able to pull the door open. Reaching in, he seizes what he's after. A manual, printed in-house, entitled *Port Computer System: A Complete User's Guide*. He scans the contents and finds what he's looking for.

Moving to the nearest terminal, he's already flicked through to the right page.

DELETING A CASE.

The screen stares at Henry, its cursor blinking away hypnotically. Pulling a high chair in behind him, Henry gets to it, following the instructions religiously. First he has to bring up the cases for the day in question. Up flashes the list of the cases that came through on Sunday, in the order in which they have been logged into the computer.

He scrolls down for an eternity, watching the roll of names

and nationalities flash before him, the infinite variety reduced to a list of refusals, removals and, of course, refugees. Henry notices the regularity with which Speerpoint's name is flagged as refusing officer.

He has no trouble remembering the name he wants deleted, the name that's been haunting him for the last three days. The times of the entries gradually get nearer to the mark, around two o'clock, he remembers. He keeps scrolling, not seeing it yet.

The computer bleeps irritably, telling him to stop pressing. He has reached the end of the list.

Henry rubs his eyes. He must have missed the entry. He scrolls back, slowly, but can't seem to locate it. He shivers. The cold is getting into his head, he presumes, cramping his brain. He goes back through them, staring hard at the screen now. It is definitely not there. There are two other entries at around the same time, but these are both female. He goes back and forward, above and beyond these two entries, but nothing is there that corresponds with his cold, unblinking passenger of Sunday.

Then he notices something strange.

Each case has a reference number generated by the computer every time an entry is made.

The cases are arranged before him in order. He notices that the two Chinese listed do not, however, have consecutive numbers.

The first, logged in at 14.26, has reference X94152.

The next, clocked six minutes later, has X94154 adjacent to it.

Henry thinks back.

X94153. That might have been it. He runs it through his head. It begins to sound very familiar.

Quickly Henry speed-reads the manual for the secret password to get into the Case Delete program and enters it. The computer asks him which case reference he wishes to take out.

X94153, he types in.

The computer pauses for a moment.

THIS CASE REFERENCE HAS ALREADY BEEN DELETED, it tells him.

Henry sits back, the chair creaking beneath him. His case has disappeared. Or perhaps not. Perhaps there has been a glitch with the computer. Maybe someone (it could easily happen) just pressed the wrong button at the wrong time. It's not like people are trained how to use it properly. Anything can go wrong. If that is the case, there would still be a file. And if there's still a file, he's going to destroy it. Shred the bastard. He wouldn't be the first . . .

He goes to the casework office to see. He checks in every filing run.

But there's no file. Without a computer log and a file, there is no case.

And there is no dodgy gook. Never has been. As if he never existed.

Henry stands in the casework office, leaning against a filing cabinet, trying to make sense of it, but his mind is freewheeling with sleepiness, thoughts form madly then scatter like a handful of dropped change. What really matters is that his name is off the records. He's in the clear. The only person who knows anything about it now is Thorough. It might have been Ed who's responsible for the whole case turning to dust. If Henry could just get something from him, the nod that he has nothing to worry about . . .

Henry enters the holding room, where he picks up two more cups of coffee out of the machine. The half-dozen or so bodies scattered around, hugging the rough blankets on offer, shuffle with the whining of the machine as it spews out. One of the dark shapes even sits up, but Henry isn't really bothered at having disturbed them. He fuels the cups with extra sugar and carries them back to the watchhouse. As he sits down again, he almost drops them with sleep. To nod off is fatal, for it is he who has to watch the flight screen and inform the rest, all snuggled up in their sleeping bags at various corners of the office, that the first flight is on its way. If he misses it, they all miss it. There are no excuses for that. He drinks one coffee quickly and blinks hard several times to try to stay awake, but as soon as he stops the clouds gather, his head lolls forward . . .

He dreams that he's dancing with Bob Gascoigne, cheek to cheek. The Bitch is wearing a gown and Henry is in full evening dress. Both have the number 189 on their backs. The music that only they can hear stops. At a table the judge sits. He raise two cards to show their score. WARNING – VIOLENT, they announce. Everyone is delighted and explodes into silent applause. The dancers take a step back from one another, Henry still holding the Bitch's shoulder, Bob's hand firmly around Henry's waist. They stare into each other for a moment, offer each other a brief smile before plunging forward, pushing their tongues into each other's mouths . . .

PrrrrrrrrrrrrrrrrrrrrrrrrrrrrrrrrrT!!!

Henry wakes at the clatter of the arrivals board, stunned.

'Huthuthu,' he says. 'Wozzar?'

The flight arrivals screen is flashing. The time is 3.12 and the ZX has just landed.

He hits the button on the Tannoy.

'ZX coming in,' he booms, taking pleasure in waking them all up, Speerpoint especially.

Five minutes later they begin to shuffle out, shoulders bent, eyes black, like giant pandas, weeks being taken off their lives by this one shift alone.

The CIOs emerge with cups of tea for themselves but nobody else. Out in the cold of the arrivals hall, it has dawned on Sandy, as well as everybody else, just how pissed he is. Small pieces of rice still nestle between his shocking teeth. His breath smells like drains. He goes down to the British desk to join

Speerpoint, gnawing on a corner of peshwary naan somebody left by the sink.

Henry steps off the watchhouse and manages to take up a position as the first punters totter in. Nigerian passengers are invariably tottering due to the amazing amounts of hand luggage they carry, more often than not comprising giant bags made of plastic twine.

Barry Venables comes down, spinning on his stump behind the line of IOs.

'Right,' he says. 'Let's keep it tight. And keep your eye out for forgeries. Aaaaaah,' he adds, breaking into his Nigerian impersonation to improve staff morale. 'Eeet eeez my pass-pot.'

It starts. Henry gets a woman, big and broad, brightly dressed in lurid green gown and head-dress. She hands over four green passports, the earliest dating back to the 1960s, all stapled together into one giant book.

'Hello, darleeeng,' she says.

'Hello,' says Henry. 'How long are you staying?'

'Who?'

'You.'

'Me?'

'You.'

She clicks her tongue. 'I don't know. Juzz a few days.'

'And what are you doing here?'

'Me? I haff com' to buy shoooz in Sho'dish.'

Shoes in Shoreditch. Or leather goods at Liverpool Street. Or car parts in Camden. Well-established responses for the negotiation of immigration, with a high success rate. Henry has no idea whether they even sell refusal shoes in Shoreditch, but he never questions it for fear of what he might discover.

What Henry is aware of above all else in this situation is that Nigerians know the ropes. Whether it's a natural talent, or one learned through osmosis after decades of shared experience, he doesn't know. But the fact is that they understand the rules of engagement across the desk better than anyone. They play it smart: the conspicuously African gear, the snowstorms of business paperwork, the massive wads of cash. An example: Henry knows that one of the giant twine bags will be full of foul-smelling dried fish. Ostensibly, she's bringing it over for a relative, but if he holds her up, then she knows he'll have to go down to Customs and get a noseful. Is that what he wants? Not on your life.

Above all, they can sniff weakness from a furlong away and exploit it, knowing just when to heighten the temperature, just when to turn the screw on an IO who has yet to eliminate all contamination of liberal humanism from his character. On a Terminal C head-hunter it doesn't matter, because by that stage they're probably as good as refused anyway. But on someone like Henry it always works.

Henry asks her a couple more questions, aware of Barry Venables lurking behind.

'Do you have a return ticket, madam?'

'Yes.'

'Can I see it?'

She chooses this moment to remind him who's the boss. 'Tcha,' she clucks, shaking her head. 'Tcha. You ask me these questions because I am black.'

'That's not true,' Henry says.

'No? You ask white people dis? No, only black skin.'

The woman hands over the ticket, knowing she's got him right where she wants him. Henry feels angry and upset, knows that the only way he can prove her wrong is by landing her. Henry looks quickly at the ticket and then, *booooomBang*, stamps her passport.

'Thank you,' he says.

She goes through, contemptuous at Henry's house-of-cards capitulation.

The flight is, mercifully, only about half-full, and Henry sees a total of around a dozen passengers, five of whom are doing the shoes in Shoreditch shuffle. He has issued no IS81s, has no cases of his own, but there are plenty of spares to go around. As soon as the last passenger is seen and, being the last passenger, sat down because his passport is a forgery, the delegation of leftovers can begin.

Speerpoint is in heated conversation with one woman, who is surrounded by a total of four children. In response to a question of his, she is wiping her hands and shaking her head.

'. . . Lizzen to me,' she says. 'I dunno anyt'ing 'bout dem. I have come for asylum. I want to know how long before I can leave here.'

Speerpoint sighs, pissed off. The blind alley of asylum work is anathema to him.

'You're not going anywhere until you tell me about the children you arrived with.'

She tuts hard and shakes her head, repeating the hand-cleaning motion.

'I don't know. They are nut'ing to do with me. I haff nut'ing to do with them. What about me?'

'Do they have any family here?'

'How should I know?'

'They were on the same passport as you.'

No reply.

'Madam, you tried to gain entry by deception, using these children in the attempt. Is that not right?'

'The passport had four chillen on it, so the agent gave me four chillen to bring. I did not ask for this.'

'What would you have done if you had got through without detection?'

'They are nut'ing to do with me. I am in fear of my life,' she adds for good measure, rummaging in her handbag.

There are twelve cases in all off the ZX. Two of these are immediate asylum claims; there are three obvious forgeries, four cases of impersonation and three 'doubtful' visitors. Three of the impostors have been picked up on the British desk. Henry would prefer one of these, as impostors are straightforward, airtight cases. But he gets lumbered with one of the forgeries, a young man, six foot eight, trendy in leather jacket and new jeans. His name, or rather the name in the passport, is Chukwunonye Ogunbiyi.

Forty-five minutes later, with the clock hands flopping at 4.40 a.m., he's still insisting it's his name.

'It is I. It is I,' he says.

Henry groans and shuts his eyelids, lead-heavy, swaying gently in the blast of the air-conditioners. Chucky's persistent mendacity has taken him to a place beyond weariness. He runs a hand through his hair, which feels greasy.

'No, arhhhhh, God, just tell me . . . look, man, I know it's duff.'

'It is what?'

'A forgery. It's a forgery.' Henry is having trouble reopening his eyes. He swallows. There is an appalling taste at the back of his throat.

Chukwunonye, or whatever his real name is, makes a grab for the passport, still in Henry's hands. Henry struggles to keep it.

'Look, come on,' he says. 'We know it's a forgery. You know it's a forgery. We know that you know it's a forgery. Everybody knows. It's a forgery, for Christ's sake. So you can't get in.'

The Nigerian looks at Henry, a certain blankness in his eyes betraying the furious thought processes that are behind it. He cocks his head and leans forward, resting elbows on the desk, looking as if he's ready to try a different tack.

Henry waits. Chukwunonye strokes the light down at the back of his head.

'There is something you must know,' he says.

'Yeeeeeeeessss . . .'

'Something that will help you in your considerations.'

'And what would that be?'

Chukwunonye sits back up and nods. 'It izz my pass-pot,' he says. 'It is I.'

'Fuck me,' groans Henry. 'Right.' He picks up the passport again. 'Look at this.'

He turns to the page of the passport which contains the photograph and personal details. The forger has pulled the laminate over the page away and then reattached it with glue, which has over time turned a telltale brown and begun to bubble under the plastic film.

'Look,' says Henry. 'Those brown marks. That's where it has been reglued so they could put your picture in. It's not very good. It's an obvious forgery.'

The man looks carefully at the brown stains for several seconds.

'I . . . may I call you by your name, sir?'

'Sorry?'

'What is your name?'

'Erm . . . Henry,' says Henry, immediately regretting it.

'Aaaaah,' he breathes out. 'Mistah Henry, I understand what you are saying, but it is for me to explain. I must tell you that Nigeria, my country,' he adds, enforcing this by punching his own chest, 'my country, has become a place of many rogues. If I walk down in the street in Abuja, where I reside, there are many men who would want to divest me of my personal affairs.

So,' he continues, raising a long finger and shaking it, 'this is why I always carry my valuables, which my passport is, in a secret place upon my person. This is the place where it turns brown. I will show you.'

He stands suddenly and begins tugging at the belt around his jeans.

'Whoa, whoa,' says Henry. 'No, no. Just sit down. Thank you. That's . . . yeah. Erm, no. Look, it's a forgery and you're not . . .'

He stops to glance down at the passport.

'Chukwunonye Ogunbiyi, Mistah Henry,' says Chukwunonye.

'Right,' says Henry. 'But it's not you. You put your picture in his passport because he had a visa. And the brown marks are from . . .'

'No, Mistah Henry, I will show you. I keep it in my inside knicker.'

In a flash he's up again, this time loosening his belt and dropping his trousers. Attached to his underwear, little more than a black posing pouch, he is patting a canvas pocket bag that is attached by a cord around his waist.

'You see, Mistah Henry. You see my inside knicker. It makes everything brown . . .'

It is, of course, at this moment that Speerpoint chooses to walk in, strolling past the glass of the interview booth, the female impostor in tow.

He stops at the doorway and looks in, sizing up the situation, the giant African, bent slightly forward over the desk in a gesture of pleading, his buttocks shining in the strip lighting, Henry facing him, looking up, mouth open.

'All right, boys?' says Speerpoint.

'We're just finishing,' says Henry.

'H'm. I can see.' He moves on with a smirk. Henry watches him go by, fantasising him pinned to the wall by a pitchfork through the neck, his toes dangling millimetres from the ground . . .

'Put your trousers on,' he says to Chukwunonye. 'You're refused.'

It's just before five when the first scheduled flights start coming in. Fatigue is dragging Henry into an almost hallucinatory state. His own voice echoes like a troglodyte chant around him. He becomes pathologically averse to eye contact. Seeing himself in a mirror in the office, his skin looks almost transparent. His sinuses feel like two wrecking balls swinging behind his eyes. And out on the control, in the freezing cold, he's certain he can hear the sound of stubble creaking its way out of his skin.

Against all this, Henry still feels the tangible pleasure of relief that the Chinese business is out of the way, that he's swerved it in the very best traditions of *cover your back* . . .

Passengers are arriving, as if conjured up by a malevolent warlock just out of sight. For most of them, the ones who do not have chartered limousines attending them, they are here only to have to wait another hour until the first Tubes and black cabs appear. There are no presenters, no queues at this time in the morning; they come from all directions.

Prrrrrrrrrrtttt

Boom

Bang

He lands everything, no questions asked.

At 7.30 a.m., thirteen and a half hours after he arrived, Henry's still around, in the main office now. At one time the night shift could have expected to be away, but a recent diktat from the Bitch means that now it's not before eight o'clock, the bitter end. He's sitting, but his upper body has flung itself on to the desk in front, both arms wrapped around his head, defending him from the erosive effects of the strip lighting and the air-conditioners.

He is not actually asleep, although a glob of saliva is trickling from the corner of his mouth. He is pretending to be asleep, literally keeping his head down while the story of Chukwunonye with his arse out in the interview room does the rounds. Henry senses it hovering above him like a swarm, gathering impetus, ready to sting.

He straightens up quickly, making himself dizzy, and rubs his eyes. Across the room, Daniella is asleep, resting her head and her soft, long hair on Speerpoint's shoulder. He is talking to Dave Niblo, quietly. Henry knows exactly what about. As soon as they see him roused, they look away. By the time Henry comes back to work tomorrow and the game of Terminal C Chinese whispers is complete, he and Chukwunonye will have been caught fisting each other on a moving baggage carousel . . .

Henry sees Ed Thorough walk in and quickly scan the room before disappearing into the forgery annexe. Henry summons up his courage to follow him in, ask him about, something to do with a case . . . Yeah, that was it, the Chinese with no visa who'd turned up on Sunday . . . needed to have a word . . . just set his mind at ease . . .

Ed disappears into the forgery room. Henry gets up and sets off after him.

. . . just pop in, poke my head around the door, just ask the question, plain and simple . . .

He grabs the handle, which rattles, and goes in.

As usual, the forgery room is dark, lit only by a feeble Angle-poise. Ed Thorough is sitting with his back to the door. He is hunched forward, disguising whatever sits before him on the desk with his formidable frame. As Henry moves to stand on the threshold, he thinks he hears a slamming noise, like that of a drawer being closed quickly.

'Ed,' says Henry.

Ed doesn't look around.

'I'm busy,' he says, hunching further forward over something, a red passport, Henry thinks, but he can't be sure.

'No, it's just . . . remember that Chinese case?'

'No.'

'Sunday. Chinese bloke. Ugly bastard. I handed him over to you. No Julius.'

Thorough shrugs, still looking the wrong way. 'Knocked him off, I suppose. Don't remember who you're talking about, though.'

'It's just that I couldn't find the file or what had happened on the computer.'

'You went looking for the file?'

'Just, you know, just to see how it panned out.'

'I told you. Knocked him off.'

'It's just that I couldn't find it on the computer, that's all . . .'

Shut up, Henry, shut up . . .

Thorough is irritated now, shakes his head, grimaces in one-quarter profile.

'Look, sprog,' he says, 'I was bouncing yellows while you were still in nappies. I don't waste my time, farting around with files or the fucking computer. I just told the little runt that he was refused and put him on the fucking plane. And fucking well keep that to yourself or I'll kick you all the way to Gate 74. All right?'

Tiredness is dulling Henry's reactions. He's thinking too slowly, feels as if the bloke standing in the doorway talking to Thorough is a third party . . .

'You know, it's just that someone must have erased him from the records—'

. . . *Shut up* . . .

Thorough turns and looks. Henry blusters. 'No, I'm not saying . . . It must just have been erased by accident or something.'

'Fuck off,' says Thorough. 'I'm busy.'

Henry pauses at the door, a part of him desperate to redeem the situation, trying to bail himself out of trouble, like a schoolchild faced with an hour's detention.

'It's just that I think I understand what's going on here. I just want to be sure that I'm in the clear, you know.'

Thorough freezes as Henry speaks, turns around slowly. 'You think you understand what's going on, do you?' he says, mockery and menace twinned in his smile.

Henry opens his mouth to speak but doesn't get the chance. Thorough is out of his chair, which topples over behind him, and is suddenly nose to nose with Henry.

'You don't understand anything. Not one fucking thing. And if you take my advice, that's the way you want to keep it. Now, fuck off.'

Henry leaves and shuts the door, teeth gritted in self-contempt. What did he expect from Thorough? Tea and sympathy? He knew the bloke was a law unto himself, MI5 spook or not. Now he'd stuck his nose in and made an exhibition of himself. Stupid, stupid, stupid . . .

He throws himself back into the same chair and shuts his eyes. At least Henry believes what Thorough said about carting the gook off to the plane, no questions asked, fast and loose behaviour entirely in keeping with his character. The gook is gone, forgotten. That, at least, is a relief.

There is a tap on his shoulder. Ronan is there, sliding into a sitting position on the desk.

'You are coming to the Allports this afternoon, aren't you?'

'Today, is it?'

'Why don't you come down?'

'No, I . . .'

'Why not?'

Henry looks into space. 'Because, erm . . . because I don't want to get kicked to death by a fat lag from Edinburgh Airport.'

'That's what it's all about, man, so it is, you soft ponce. You've got to get in there, give as good as you get. I've heard there's a few chiefies playing. Wouldn't you love to chop one of those bastards down, grind your studs right in their face, like in a proper Irish sport? Wouldn't that make you feel good?'

'I haven't got any boots.'

'Well, look, just come down for a pint after. It'll be a crack, man.'

'Ah, Ronan . . .'

'Just come down for a pint with me, later on. That's all I'm asking.'

'All right, all right.'

'Brilliant,' says Ronan, showing Henry the file he's carrying. 'You were dealing with this—' he looks at the front '—Chucky-fucky, weren't you?'

'Yeah. What's happening with him?'

'What's happening with him?' laughs Ronan, speaking loudly. 'Well, he's standing up in the middle of the pen with his trousers round his ankles asking for Mistah Henry.'

Everybody laughs. Everybody knows. Speerpoint's told everybody.

'Thanks a lot,' sneers Henry.

Ronan taps him gently on the head with the file.

'Oh, and he's played his joker. So he won't be leaving. Should I be giving him your phone number?'

Henry falls asleep twice at the wheel on the drive home, which is about average. Once in bed, he sleeps uneasily for five hours, waking once and for all at two o'clock in the afternoon when Chocolate mugs him for lunch.

After a shower, he makes himself a bacon and chutney sandwich and eats it slowly, staring out of the window, watching the sky darken, the Bitch's question rattling in his mind.

What is it that you want *from life?*

What is it that you want from life?

What is it that YOU *want from life?*

Henry gets his coat and heads to the West End.

He dozes fitfully along the imperial purple of the Piccadilly Line, finally creeping out of Leicester Square Station like a rodent who has forgotten to hibernate.

Turning up Charing Cross Road, down Little Newport Street and into Soho, shuffling around between gangs of Algerian and Albanian refugees killing time between dole cheques, he looks at the faces around him in a way he once would never have dreamed of.

. . . See him? He's a Kenyan, possibly Sudanese, definitely not Somali, take it from me . . . Korean over there, easy to tell the difference, different skin tone from a Jap . . . Now, then, fat bloke, dressed in Pakistani garb, but Gulf features, maybe a Syrian, no, Afghan, I'll go for Afghan . . . That bloke up the back alley, pissing on to his own shoes, he'll be from Manchester . . .

Henry hates this game, but it is impossible not to play. He longs for the naivety of his previous life, when he didn't pick them out one by one like a demented ornithologist, clutching his *Observer Book of Scrotes and Duffers.*

The change jangles louder in his pocket as he passes an amusement arcade on the edge of Chinatown. Always prepared to gamble as a short-term fix from boredom, he goes inside and drops a pound into a fruit machine.

Around him, gooks chatter and pursue their love-affair with the fruities, some standing, legs apart, feeding two, even three of the devourers at once.

Henry gets four presses of a large plastic button for his pound. Presumably he is content with this deal, for he allows another to roll between forefinger and thumb and into the slot of temptation.

As the coin drops, he looks up. To his left are a wall of mirrors, giving the illusion of greater space. They afford him a view of the other side of the arcade, behind the machine he is facing.

He recognises someone, pouring pound coins into a machine with a tattooed hand. A star tattoo . . .

Recognises . . .

Recognises . . .

Oh, shit!

It's him.

It's fucking Xiao!

Henry blushes and leaves, head ducked.

He's convinced he's been seen, *he fucking knows it.*

WARNING – VIOLENT, he sees when he blinks.

Henry keeps walking, hands deep in his jacket pockets, making tight turns at corners. He doesn't dare to look back. *Xiao, that was his name, Jesus Christ, Nasty-looking bastard. Don't look back. Don't look . . .*

Henry makes a half-turn as he passes a dark shop window to see if he can get a glimpse of Xiao in the reflection, but he can't tell. He hears a Chinese voice behind him, jabbering. That'll be him, that'll be him on his mobile, rounding up his friends, thinks Henry, fear suddenly giving him the ability to understand Mandarin. I don't want to be cut to pieces, I don't want to be dim sum . . .

WARNING.

He's running now, running, fists in both pockets of his jacket.

VIOLENT.

He remembers the cold menace in Xiao's silence and hurries even more.

WARNING.

Have to get off the street, have to get away, somewhere where I won't stand out.

The cinema. He was surrounded by cinemas. No time to be picky. Just duck in and get out of sight.

He turns right and sees one. The Prince Charles, a rerun theatre.

Straight to the box office.

'One for the next show, please.' *Don't care what it is. Don't care.*

He pays, looks back over his shoulder, no sign of him, then on, through the double doors, up the set of stairs and away, back to the furthest corner of the auditorium where only a dozen or so sit in clumps of one or two. He slides himself down hard into a seat, barely able to see above the one in front. He tries to breathe deeply but his shoulders are knotted in fear, his stomach swinging like a punch-bag.

He quakes as a new head pokes into the pink gloom and looks around for somewhere to sit, but no death squad of gooks appears.

The lights go down. The curtains part. The censor's classification looms before him.

The Piano. He's walked into a screening of *The Piano.*

'Oh, no,' he says, out loud.

Twenty minutes of *The Piano* and Henry's ready to take his chances with the Triads.

He stumbles down the cold, dank fire exit, bursting through the doors and out into the twilight.

Nobody there.

chapter 4

friendly fire

Thursday – Early Shift

Henry stares at the clock on the office wall, his eyelids threatening to drop and obscure it. Only now, after a sleepless night, does he feel tired.

4.55 a.m.

His shift begins in five minutes.

Having gone straight home the day before, Jerome away God knows where, the solitude has allowed his imagination to whisk itself into paranoia. What if he was seen? Or followed? What if they followed him and were just waiting outside for him? That was absurd, but still he kept the lights off all night. Then, as the night had drawn on, his fear began to redirect itself towards his return to work. He expected something to happen, the Bitch or Hammond to be waiting for him with a sick, knowing smile. It was the very vagueness of his fear that made it so unpleasant. He contemplated calling in sick, but that just meant condemning himself to more worry. Of course, as he realises now, there was nothing to worry about. He came in to work and was elated at the general uninterest on his entrance.

Sitting in the staff room now, facing the forgery room door, he feels calm enough to piece it together in his mind. Thorough must have been around waiting for the Chinese with no visa. He was lurking outside, tipped off that Xiao was coming. Something prearranged, something organised. When he got held up, the gook ended up with Henry. Maybe he intended to just stamp up the passport he had with something appropriate, or (more likely) there was a different document waiting for him. Who knows, it might have been happening for the tenth, for the hundredth time? He wonders how much they pay him, whoever *they* are, for this service. He wonders who Thorough has got himself embroiled with. Chinese crims have the reputation of being just about the nastiest around.

Henry sees now that he screwed things up big time when he put the gook's details on the computer. Obviously the matter wasn't supposed to go that far. So Ed removed the entry himself.

The upshot? One more dodgy gook in London? *What the hell do I care?*

One thing preys on his mind. Knowing what he knows now, he would never have approached Thorough as he did yesterday. He understands now why Thorough had reacted, and it was food for thought.

And not for the first time, Henry clutches his own temple, grits his teeth with the thought that he'd told Thorough that he knew what was going on . . .

Shit!

Just keep quiet and *cover your back, cover your back . . .*

No problem, thinks Henry. Xiao didn't even see me. No problem.

The relief that he's got away with it actually makes him feel upbeat, even though it's five to five in the bloody morning and the air-conditioners are flaying him alive.

Elsewhere in the room, the rest of the A shift sit, mostly in silence, eyes trained down on cups of coffee or ahead into space. A few have their eyes shut, brows stretched, taunted by the unrewarding margins of sleep. Only Sid Bennison, five foot nothing, wearing one of the golf sweaters that comprise his entire wardrobe, standing in the corner practising his swing, isn't knackered. He was in bed at eight o'clock last night, in preparation for his daily thirty-six holes after work.

Henry rubs his face, trying to loosen up the flesh on his cheeks, unnaturally tight, being sucked off his skull by the air-conditioners. Inside his head, his own touch on his own skin, nails scraping stubble, sounds like a brutal deforestation.

The uneasy silence is clattered into by a noise from the corridor outside.

'*Bar-sterd*!'

Jimmy Craddock has dropped one of his crutches.

'*BAR-sterd!*'

The door smashes open. Jimmy insists on doing A shifts, against medical advice, the main benefit being the extra time it gives him to pursue his thriving death wish.

'Can someone get my bar-*sterd* crutch?' he shouts.

A new girl, nearest the door, gets up. By assisting him, she gives Jimmy the chance to grab a handful of arse.

'Thank you, darling,' he says, hobbling further down the corridor to the smoking room for a ciggy.

Henry looks back at the clock, as if it is going to tell him something other than the fucking time.

One minute to five.

The Tannoy speaks. '*All right, ladies and gentlemen of the A shift. Five o'clock. Let's have you all out.*'

Outside, a few sagging bodies man the border – this is the skeleton night staff, where Henry was yesterday, eleven hours behind them and three agonising hours to go. At five in the morning, the arrivals control is shivery-cold. Officers hug mugs of tea between passengers or sit hunched with cardigans around their shoulders.

The A shift come out gingerly, like coma cases renewing their acquaintance with consciousness. The general antisociability of the hour means that they sit apart from one another.

The exception to this rule is Jimmy Craddock, who has, at the first call, shot out, lit fag hanging from bottom lip and swung himself on his sticks to the desks before anybody else. He takes up his customary position, known as Jimmy's Chair, which just happens to be situated so that a wide supporting metal pillar obstructs the watchhouse's view of him.

There are those upstairs who marvel at Jimmy's will to come to work, what with all his problems, who cite his dedication, his bloody die-hard commitment to the job. It's not a job to Jimmy, they say; it's a fucking way of life.

There is a beautiful irony in this. The real reasons why Jimmy wants that chair are twofold. First, it allows him the succour of his hip flask whenever he feels the need. Secondly, it means nobody standing in the watchhouse can see him while he accumulates his second income, taking 'airport taxes' at £10 a time from slopes and Yanks of gullible character.

Henry gets into a chair and hunches forward over the desk.

The first flights are all from the Far East: Malaysia, Singapore, Hong Kong, Indonesia, Thailand, Taiwan.

The hall is eerie, almost unreal. The cold silence has a whining quality, like a dog whistle, keeping everything in check. The atmosphere is one of quiet industry, even the chorus of stamps on desks more studious. Few questions are asked, and those that are asked are designed to lead towards landing. The onus is strictly on getting people through, which suits Henry fine. For the head-hunters, this is a bad time. If you're duff, a stone-cold, duff-as-fuck knock-off, this period gives you just about your best chance to make it over the line. Anything on the margin gets the benefit. Head-hunters don't do A shifts very often, preferring to come with the Bs a couple of hours later, when things are calmer and you can take your time, play the queue, pluck one out . . .

Away to the right and happily obscured sits Jimmy Craddock. He knows that the chiefies on duty now are the ones who have overseen the night duty (not for them, getting out of their comfortable beds at half-past three in the fucking morning) and that they are in the watchhouse, half-asleep, talking shit, shoes off, stretching their sore feet with no prospect of coming out to walk the control. So he happily gets on with his work, punctuated by regular libations from his hip flask. As Henry looks over, he can see him poring through a Taiwanese tourist's wallet, deftly extracting a twenty-pound note in exchange for a stamp in his passport. The tourist seems satisfied with this transaction and lifts his hat in thanks.

If Jimmy is charging double his normal rate, that usually means he's planning on only doing a half-day.

Beyond Jimmy, Sid Bennison stamps quietly, a smile dancing on his face as he envisages the middle of the fairway at the seventeenth, dodging the bunkers, avoiding the rough.

Behind the assorted slopes come more slopes and then, at about six, the first All-America flight drops on to tarmac. Flights from the West Coast first, closely followed by passengers from Chicago, Orlando, Washington, JFK, Newark (not the same as New York), Dallas, Boston. Americans collide with the backs of queues and talk about it, raising the general volume. Gradually, mysteriously, stamps begin to come down harder. *Boombangabangboom.* The flow of movement, languid and regular before, becomes hectic, staccato. The hall becomes competitive. Rogue opportunists, usually 'here on business' types, sneak down the side and walk along the line of desks, waiting for a soft spot. Their temerity is not missed by the queue.

'Hey, buddy, get in the goddam line!' shouts one.

The offender, a fat guy who is by the law of averages an

average lawyer, blushes but pretends to ignore. He goes through immediately.

They all go through immediately. They think the questions are pleasantries. They're right.

'How long are you staying?'

'Well, how nice of you to ask . . .'

To Henry's displeasure, a squat, dumpy presence installs itself into the desk next to him. It is Malcolm Cartwright, mid-forties, clad in immaculate three-piece suit, starched collar, regimental tiepin, hair painstakingly symmetrical, small grey moustache brushed down as per regulations. *Malcolm's* regulations.

Malcolm is late, even with his watch synchronised to air-traffic control time, which he follows illegally on his own short-wave radio. This, the being late part, is, under Malcolm's own regulations, unforgivable. But there are mitigating circumstances. Since being dishonourably discharged from the marital home by the second Mrs Cartwright three months ago and becoming technically homeless, Malcolm has had to fall back on all his Para training. He effectively lives in his Land Rover in the staff car park, sleeping there and cooking himself protein-rich tinned meals over a camper stove. He performs his exhaustive toilet in the airside public lavatories, hogging one of the sinks for half an hour as he clips, combs, brushes and lays on the Trumper's Gentleman's Hair Tonic.

Malcolm lifts himself up into his chair and casts a look across the ebb and flow of the morning's arrivals.

'Bloody cattle,' he says. 'Don't want stamping. Want bloody branding. Like animals.'

He pauses, suddenly thoughtful, melancholy even.

'Beautiful sunrise this morning,' he says.

Henry looks across at him involuntarily. The artificial light is reflecting a strange film over Malcolm's eyes as he stares ahead. For a moment Henry feels wretched with sorrow for him.

It passes, and the next herd of Americans stampede towards them.

Henry gets an elderly couple. Mr and Mrs Duwayne Thigpen, no less.

'Howdy, son,' says Mr Thigpen, pulling up his trousers. He is wearing a black cap with a design in gold braid and 'Fightin' 45s' written on it.

'What will you be doing in the UK?' Henry asks.

'Army reunion,' says Mr Thigpen, tapping his headgear. 'I was here during the war. The war, right? When we saved your limey ass.'

Henry looks up, thinking he's joking. He's not joking, but he is incredibly pissed. Henry glances at Mrs Thigpen, who is quite obviously doped up to the eyeballs.

'That's right, sonny. You got yourselves in too deep and we had to come in and pull your limey butts out of the goddam fire—'

Henry quickly stamps and hands the passports back, gesturing for them to go through.

'Thank you, sugar,' says Mrs Thigpen slowly. 'Oh, God.' She turns to her husband. 'Duwayne, I can't move my legs.'

'Sure you can, honey. Sure you can. One step at a time, that's right . . .' He looks again at Henry as they move past, his wife clinging desperately to him. 'Yessir, you limey bastards got lucky the day we came into the show. If we hadn't saved—'

From the next desk, Malcolm pipes up. 'I rather think it's the Russians we should thank.'

'Beg your pardon? You wanna repeat that?'

'I was merely pointing out,' reiterates Malcolm, keen military historian, 'that it would probably be more accurate to thank the Soviet Union for saving us. The Eastern Front, you know, sapping the German war machine.'

Mr Thigpen is not having it. 'Now you listen to me, you little prick. Of all the ungrateful sons of bitches—'

Outraged, he waves a long, liver-spotted finger at Malcolm. In so doing, he leaves Mrs Thigpen without support. She falls backwards and tumbles. With a grim inevitability, her wig is dislodged, sliding forward over her face and on to her lap. The artificial light gleams cruelly on her bald head.

'Oh,' she says from the floor. 'Oh. Oh.'

Quickly, they are joined by some other members of the Fightin' 45s geriatric entourage.

'You got a problem there, Duwayne?' asks one.

'What I got is a goddamn commie-loving piece o' shit asshole who ought t' ha' been gassed with the rest of his kind. Next time—' he gives it to Malcolm again '—we'll let you motherfuckers rot.'

'If I may say so, sir,' Malcolm responds. 'That kind of language does you and the unit whose insignia you bear no credit whatsoever.'

'You fuck . . . you, God, if I had my fucking gun, I'd shoot you like the yellow dog you are!'

'Just walk away, Duwayne,' says one of his fellow veterans. 'He's just trying to provoke you. Just walk away . . .'

'Duwayne!' wails Mrs Thigpen. 'Have you got my pills? I think I broke my back.'

'No, you didn't, honey,' replies her husband, hauling her up by the armpits and slapping her syrup of fig back on. 'You just think you did.'

'Can I still have the pills?' she says as he leads her away.

'Sure you can, honey . . .'

Malcolm shakes his head, straightens his tie.

'You know what they call that, don't you? Friendly fire. More dangerous than the bloody enemy.'

The Wallaby Airlines drops as the B shift begins to make its way out. The coincidence of the first antipodean flights landing and the B shift coming on duty is a happy one for the senior head-hunters, for no nationality walks into being refused like Australians; nobody just stands there and asks for it like they do. In this case, Henry understands what sticks in the head-hunter's craw. The truth is they think they own the fucking place. And nobody likes to see that.

Sid Bennison's got one. Female, blonde, a little butch, already nursing a nice melanoma. She is in her citizen-of-the-world uniform – grey T-shirt with frayed collar, combat shorts, walking boots and thick socks (just great for air travel), Dick Whittington handkerchief knotted around her neck and shoe-laces tied to her wrists.

Sid's other hobby, beside golf, is taking out backpackers. He's been at it for more than twenty years. At one time he might have been convinced that this was the best way to get the promotion he craved, but now he just does it for fun. For years he applied for inclusion in the Chiefies' Curse and every year he got knocked back. This trend is the source of a great deal of resentment among a certain generation of staff, all male, who feel their 'porridge' is being ignored. Sid's resentment is palpable but tends to be misdirected at anyone under the age of twenty-five with a rucksack and an uncontrollable desire to see the world. For Sid and his ilk, the dirtiest word in the English language is 'student'.

He glances through the passport.

'How long you staying?' he asks, smiling, nice and pally.

The blonde shrugs.

'Ah, dunno. You know, I've just come for a while, check out the place. Just bummin' around, you know how it is.'

Sid doesn't.

'You'd better take a seat, love,' he says.

Refused. Asking for it, quite frankly. Henry looks on with a tiny nod of approval.

*

A lull follows, half an hour of calm between Americans and the rest of the species.

In the office, the rattle of chatter centres around one subject.

'It was only the third game of the tournament. Terminal D versus Glasgow Airport. I'm not kidding you, man. The ref blows his whistle and they're right into it, all twenty-two of them. The ball didn't leave the centre spot. One of the fucking Jocks – they've got their faces painted like last year – one of the Jocks has taken his boots off and he's swinging them around his head like what'chacallit? . . .'

'A mace?'

'Nah, not really. Them South American things they swing around their heads and stot people with.'

'Yeah. I know what you mean. Dunno what they're called.'

'Yeah. Thingies.'

'Yeah.'

All around the room and beyond, the tale of the Allports is spun. Behind the sound of tongues clicking in disapproval, there is a sense of amused resignation to this kind of thing.

' . . . Boys will be boys . . .'

' . . . Any of ours get arrested?'

'You know Ronan? He turned up with his mush painted green. Got sent off in our first game for stamping, had to be pulled off the pitch. When the scrap started on the other pitch, he just got stuck in with them.'

'What side was he on?'

'I don't think he was worried about that . . .'

Philip Heffer comes in carrying two well-used blue passports.

'Look what the cat dragged in,' he says.

'What?'

'The Fleisches.'

Cue much groaning and puffing of cheeks.

This is not the first time the Fleisches have come, she

hobbling on two sticks, wearing a shimmering henna wig and cardboard-thick lipstick, he cross-eyed, the crotch of his trousers level with his knees, smelling like a dog.

Heffer counts out loud a total of nine refusal stamps between them. Normally they travel together, always for the same purpose.

They have come to kill the Queen. Indeed, this is their lives' work, born, as they explain, from an atavistic feud over land around the time of Charlemagne. Mrs Fleisch is a keen genealogist and has traced the House of Windsor back to a family of notorious cattle smugglers in what is now western Poland. It goes without saying that the ancient family of Fleisch were among their victims, but you don't mess with the Fleisches and expect to get through the next 1,200 years unscathed. From a stationary recreational vehicle in Omaha, they have plotted an inevitable revenge, which always falters at the first hurdle when they are asked why they have come and they tell the truth. One thing about the Fleisches: never less than honest.

Henry has had the pleasure of being present during a previous baggage search of the family Fleisch and even he was disconcerted by the glossy photographs of the Duke of Edinburgh with eyes cut out and the crude voodoo doll of the Princess Royal, legs akimbo.

Henry feels a tremor of fear as he sees Ed Thorough come in, dressed in the usual black, and walk through the office. Reassuringly, he pays Henry no notice, but it's not often that he passes Jimmy Craddock without a word, as he does today. Jimmy is, however, not so remiss.

'Here, *Ed-ward*, I was thinking of nipping down to the van for a bacon sarnie. Coming?'

Ed stops.

'No,' he says. 'Got something on.'

Jimmy looks slightly bemused as he clambers back up on his crutches. 'What'cha talking 'bout? Come down wiff me and grab a bacon sarnie. C'mon, mate, bacon sarnie, bacon *sar*-nie, mate.'

'I'm all right,' says Ed. 'Maybe later. I've got this job to do. It's for Bob Gascoigne.'

The Bitch asks him to do jobs. That's different. Besides which, Jimmy's need for cholesterol with which to clot the alcohol coursing through his system is now at desperate pitch. He gives up. At no point does he offer to get Ed, or anyone else for that matter, a bacon sarnie.

Sid Bennison comes in from his baggage search of the Australian girl, holding aloft a thick, floral-bound book.

'Got her diary,' he announces.

This causes a general interest among the other men in the room.

'Give us a look when you're finished,' says one.

'Read out the good stuff,' says another.

'She's been having a fair old time,' says Sid, flicking through. 'Little scrubber.'

Dave Niblo has picked up her passport and is looking at her picture.

'She's quite nice,' he says. 'Almost as nice as that Colombian girl who sucked me cock.'

Dave's South American blowie in the interview room on nights happened over two years ago, but he rarely lets it go unmentioned for an entire shift. Henry doubts, in fact he knows, that it's not an isolated incident – there are enough IOs who now have domestic arrangements with one-time immigration cases – but everybody except Dave appreciates the prudence of maintaining a degree of silence. The point is that his brief encounter with a pair of glossy Latino lips was the high point of his career, not to say his entire life, so it's fair enough.

At least, as he would tell you, he had the decency to land her afterwards.

When they're training you for the job, they often make reference to the possibility of passengers offering sexual favours to enter the UK.

But Henry's still waiting.

Philip Heffer approaches him, looking strung out.

'Sorry to ask you . . .' he begins. This is ominous. It implies a shitty job and Philip knows that Henry's lag sensibility is not sufficiently developed to tell him to fuck off. 'I need you to do me a favour . . .'

'What?' asks Henry, worried.

Philip bites his lip.

'I have to go and see the Bitch,' he says, putting a hand to his mouth, bending at the knees.

'Why?'

'I don't know. I don't have a fucking clue!'

Henry tries to look concerned, but in truth he's just glad it's not him.

'So what do you want me to do?'

'I had these two Americans . . .'

'Not the fuckin' Fleisches?'

'Sorry . . .'

Five minutes later, Henry is in the Customs area, standing well back as the Fleisches' bags are opened up. Like other black people in his job, with its inevitable racial complications, the Customs officer performing the task makes a careful show of studied professionalism, disguising himself in procedure, playing it by the book, which he appears to have learned backwards. He asks the stock questions (where have you come from, are you carrying any drugs, guns, animals? etc.) as if reciting the shipping forecast. Each answer he registers with a sage nod of the head. He takes his work seriously, which makes Henry simultaneously contemptuous and jealous. That said, when the fateful moment arrives and the first Fleisch bag is opened, Henry notices the step back in horror as the stench slams into his nosehairs.

The Fleisches stand, looking on. She is leaning on two sticks, as usual, massive Jewish nose keeping up plastic-rimmed, square spectacles with tinted lenses. Her henna wig has seen better days now. Her son hovers at her shoulder, eyes crossed, face marked with mysterious dark scabs, hair and rabbinical beard knotted into unwashed clumps. He breathes exclusively through his mouth, which is always open.

'What'cha doing that for? What'cha doing that for?' asks Mrs Fleisch. 'What'cha doing that for?'

'I am a Customs officer,' explains the Customs officer. 'I am inspecting your bags at the request of the Immigration Officer.'

Henry looks down. Don't get me involved, he thinks.

Mrs Fleisch is satisfied with this until the moment Customs begins to empty the first suitcase.

'What'cha doing that for?' she asks. 'What'cha doing that for?'

Fleisch *fils* steps forward. 'This,' he says in his disconcerting whisper, blinking hard, 'is a violation of my constitutional rights.'

'You don't have any constitutional rights here,' says Henry.

'My rights are—' Henry doesn't catch the last word, his attention distracted by something flying out of his beard.

The Customs officer has pulled out a folded white towel, streaked with natural browns, with something wrapped inside it. He places it down with a metallic clang and begins to unfurl, no doubt grateful for the tight rubber gloves he's wearing.

'What'cha doing that for?' asks Mrs Fleisch. 'What'cha doing that for?'

From within the towel, he produces two giant knives, which he holds up in awe. They are garishly ornate, like Spanish souvenir letter-openers, and, unlike everything else the

Fleisches touch, they are immaculately clean, polished to a gleam. And sharp.

'What are these?' asks the Customs officer, more than a hint of concern in his voice.

'They are ceremonial daggers,' explains Mr Fleisch, deadpan. 'They belong to me. I don't like you touching them. They have an . . . ordained function.'

'What function, exactly?'

Mrs Fleisch raises a stick and clatters it against the tabletop.

'What'cha think, you bozo? They're for stabbing her goddamn eyes out!'

The Customs man looks at Henry. 'Who's she talking about?'

Henry steps forward and pushes one of the Fleisches' plastic bags towards him.

'Take a look in the scrapbooks,' he says.

The Customs man pulls one out and begins to leaf through it. 'What the fuck?' he whelps, dropping it on the floor and swallowing hard.

Henry raises an eyebrow. 'Don't worry,' he says. 'They're not stopping.'

Henry makes short work of knocking off the Fleisches – he only has to copy the work of the refusals they've already had. Once all the actions are completed on the computer, it only remains for him to endorse their passports with refusal stamps. This is simply done by a normal stamp with a cross through it. Someone once came up with the nickname of Hot Cross Bun for this endorsement and, alas, it stuck.

Henry gathers all the papers and puts them on the file, then goes to his pigeonhole, where he left his stamp.

But it's not there.

Must have left it out on a table, he thinks. Soon he's scurrying, looking around, checking numbers, asking everyone to see if they've picked it up by mistake.

Nobody has. He recalls Philip's similar predicament, wishes the boot were on the other foot again.

He ventures out on to the control, quiet now, and tries to nonchalantly walk its length, checking if it's been left out.

It hasn't.

Prrrrrrrrrt

Flights are coming in. Henry grits his teeth, starts to feel flushed with anxiety.

He needs that stamp.

He tries retracing his steps, back to Customs, then up to the casework office, back out on the control. In the office, everyone recognises his problem but quietly ignores him, leaving him to his fate. Ed Thorough exits the forgery room, hands stuffed into the pockets of his leather jacket and returns a few minutes later, glassy-eyed.

Henry breathes deeply, tries to relax. *Don't need this. Not now.* It has to be somewhere. Has to be . . .

And then, just as concern begins to flirt with crisis, Dave walks in, waving Henry's stamp.

'This yours?' he asks.

'Yeah. Thank God. Where was it?'

'You'd left it down in the tea room, Mistah Henry.' Dave laughs at his reference. Henry pretends to ignore it.

'I haven't been down the tea room.'

'That's where it was.'

Henry shrugs, just happy to have it back.

He sets about stamping the Fleisches' passports to endorse their refusal.

BoomBoom

Looking down at his handiwork, he notices something strange.

The date.

The date is wrong.

He's sure he stamped on for the right date this morning. But it's been changed, like Philip's was. To the twenty-ninth. Nine days away.

And there's something else. Looking down at the Fleisches' passport pages, he can see his passport stamp number, 189, looking back up at him. That's not supposed to happen. That's why he has the strip of sellotape over it. He looks at the face of the stamp.

Someone's taken it off.

From nowhere, a sense of impending doom disorientates him. His mind flickers with facts, all of which he understands to be connected, but on which he cannot impose a definitive order.

As it happens, events are on hand to give him a nudge.

In the room behind him, a rumpus enters. Philip Heffer is at its head, his cheeks a brilliant red, his mouth tight. With him are two others. One of them is Tony de Carlo, representative of the local union branch, dressed in the white shirt with buttoned-down epaulettes he always wears, armpits stiff and brown, a line of black pens protruding from his breast pocket. The third is none other than the Bitch himself, shoulders back, head up, who walks stiffly to the lockers.

'Which one is yours?' he asks Philip.

Philip points.

'Open it.'

'There's no need to be so rude,' says Philip, looking around. Everyone else in the room is, of course, transfixed.

'You will open your locker,' snarls the Bitch.

Tony de Carlo takes off his thick-rimmed glasses and polishes them on his white shirt. 'I think we should all try to remain civil, Bob,' he says, looking down to breathe on the lenses before giving them another polish.

'I remind you,' the Bitch replies, 'that you are only here to observe and that, as senior officer at the terminal, I will supervise this search. Is that understood?'

Tony de Carlo is giving his eyes a good rub. 'Quite clear, thank you.'

Philip puts the key in the lock.

'You're both witnessing this?' he says.

'Hang on,' says Tony de Carlo. 'Can't see a thing without my bloody glasses on.'

Henry has spun around in his chair. He hears the door to the forgery room, behind him now, open.

Philip turns the key and opens the door.

'There,' he says, pushing back the curl of hair that has dropped over his eye.

'Stand back,' the Bitch exhorts. He throws both hands in and begins to rummage around. Philip folds his arms and pouts his displeasure.

'Ridiculous,' he mutters. 'I've a good mind to call my sol—'

'Is this what we're looking for?' the Bitch says.

From within the grey locker, he extracts an A4 manila envelope, which he peers into. Spinning on his heels, he turns it upside down and allows its contents to pour on to the nearest desk.

Passports. Red and brown. Chinese. Four in total. And money, dollars, a bundle of hundred-dollar bills.

Philip's hands go straight to his mouth and he buckles at the knees.

'Oh, Jesus Christ . . . This is . . .' he says. 'No . . . I've never . . .'

The Bitch is leafing through one of the passports. He holds a page open for Tony de Carlo to see.

'Endorsed,' he commentates. 'For the twenty-sixth. Seven days hence. I think we're beginning to get the picture here.'

Tony de Carlo responds with a gentle sigh. The Bitch turns again to Philip.

'This is your stamp number, I take it.'

'It's my number, but anyone could have . . . The other day . . . it went missing. I . . .'

'You are hereby suspended as an Immigration Officer pending disciplinary and possible criminal action for facilitation of illegal entrants into the United Kingdom. You will hand over your warrant.'

Philip has regained a touch of composure and reaches into his jacket pocket.

'I have never seen that—' he looks down at the evidence '— in my life before.' And with that he flings his warrant at the Bitch's feet.

Tony de Carlo is looking down, his chin doubling as he inspects his tie. He licks a finger and rubs at it.

'Best not to say anything right now,' he says. 'Keep your counsel. There are precedents. The union has a mechanism. We'll go through all the channels, don't worry.'

'You will now be escorted off the premises,' the Bitch says, coming forward and grabbing Philip by the elbow.

'Get'cha hands off me!' he screams, stamping his foot. 'Get'cha filthy hands off me. Bitch!' he screams and walks out, the Bitch a few paces behind, clutching the money and passports in his puffy white hand.

Everyone left behind waits a few seconds in silence until the coast is clear.

'Come on, then, Tony,' shouts Jimmy Craddock, picking up the discarded envelope and having a look in before dropping it himself. 'What was all that about?'

Tony de Carlo sits on the edge of one of the desks with a sigh and scratches at his thinning hair.

'Oh, I dunno. Well, I mean, you saw for yourself. I get called along to Bob's office. I just thought he wanted to talk about health and safety, you know, the dodgy door to the blokes' toilets, and before I know it he's on about organised crime.'

'Who would have thought it, eh?' says Sid Bennison.

It doesn't surprise Malcolm Cartwright. 'Not with his sort. They're anti-establishment by nature, mincing and prissing about. Burgess and Maclean all over again. Always open to blackmail as well. Probably got caught in a public lavatory with his arse out.'

'Now, now, fellers,' says Tony de Carlo. 'Innocent until proven guilty and all that. Mind you . . .' he adds, casting a look across at Philip's locker, the door still hanging open.

'How did he know?'

Tony de Carlo lifts up a foot and inspects the sole of his shoe, unhappy with something he sees there. 'Bob just put it to him, said he had reason to believe that he'd been up to no good and that he was giving him the chance to confess first . . . Mind you, he did say something interesting.'

'What was that?'

'Well, he said that about giving him a chance to confess and then he says . . . no, wait a minute . . . what he said was . . . the chance for him *or anyone he was in league with* to confess. That was it. He seemed to know something he wasn't letting on.'

The others glance at one another. Things go a little quiet.

'You think he was in with Onions, do you?'

Tony clasps his hand to the back of his neck and looks up to the polystyrene ceiling tiles with a heroic sigh.

'You know, there again, we shouldn't jump to conclusions . . .'

'Disgrace to the service,' adds Jimmy, at the end of his A-shift, finishing off counting out his wad of morning tenners under the desk.

Henry turns back around in his chair. In front of him the forgery room door is open. Standing on its threshold, looking out, one hand stretched up leaning on the lintel, is Ed Thorough.

Thorough's looking straight at Henry, straight down his

throat. Instinctively, Henry reaches out a hand and takes firm hold of his stamp, knowing that it's already too late.

'Edward,' says Jimmy. 'Ed-*ward*. You missed a right little drama there.'

'I saw it,' says Thorough, still focused on Henry. 'Who would have thought it?'

'What you up to, Edward, my boy? You still busy? How 'bout a quick little snifter down the embarks bar? Little snifter, Ed-*ward*, little snift-*er*? Celebrate my transfer to Sandgate. Celebrate them putting me out to grass. Little snif-*ter* would be in order.'

'Why not?' says Thorough. 'All this excitement's made me thirsty.'

Henry watches them leave. As soon as they're out, and as discreetly as is possible, he slips into the forgery room. Somehow he knows he won't find what he's looking for, not even knowing quite what that is anyway. But he goes in, standing in the dark room, breathing hard. In theory, any and every IO has access, but it's Thorough's domain. When he's not there, the place retains his odour, that unique whiff of leather and rolling tobacco. Hurriedly, he tries the drawers to the desk, his mind racing anew, trying to join the dots between the facts as he knows them.

It boils down to one simple chain of events.

Heffer's stamp goes missing and it winds up furnishing the forged passports of a bunch of gook crooks.

Henry sticks his nose in where it's not wanted, says, *Oh God*, says he knows what's going on . . .

Henry's stamp goes missing . . . *Christ!*

Thorough's been supplying documents for the illegals he's assisting into the country and using other IOs' stamps to endorse them to cover his tracks.

And the next number to come up . . .

The top drawer is locked. Henry pulls hard, tries to rip the fucker out. But it won't budge.

Henry furrows his brow, grits his teeth, bangs his forehead with the knuckles of one hand, trying to think. He knows that, with a will, it's no problem to get into someone else's locker, plant anything you want. A set of spare keys is kept in the duty office. Henry decides the first thing to do is to remove the one to his locker. There were almost certainly others, but it might buy him a little time.

Henry struggles to formulate his course of action. He realises that time is short, that the veiled threat was already there in the Bitch's comment to Philip about accomplices and Thorough's uncompromising stare. The Bitch was already primed to think that others were involved, so he'd be looking out for it. One hint from Thorough would be enough for Henry to find himself the next one stitched up. And no doubt Henry's stamp number is gracing the pages of the manufactured evidence already.

Henry knows that he has to change the odds in his favour. Ronan would be the obvious choice for help, but his youthful exuberance has probably still got him in the nick while the law try to pin any number of IRA atrocities on him. He knows he has to talk to somebody and that the somebody he has in mind might not be the most apparent option . . .

He asks around and learns that his quarry is in the CIOs' office, a large room halfway down the corridor towards the Bitch's office. Knocking on the open door, he goes in.

There are at Terminal C a number of people, perhaps a majority, that Henry would admit under the influence of sodium pentathol that he disliked. But in his own, extensive, roll call of unpopularity, the person he consistently despises most, the person whose attitudes are most at odds with his own, the person whose behaviour seems most carefully designed to frustrate and enrage him, the person he would most readily leave unassisted in a pool of quicksand is Chief Immigration Officer Ralph Hammond. Yet, paradoxically, he is the person he can best trust. The job is all Hammond has. Without it and the gas of petty authority he inflates himself with, he would be an even bigger zero than he already is. That's why he cares, cares enough to serve Henry's purpose.

Whatever else he thinks about him, when it comes to the good name of the Immigration Service, Henry knows that Hammond is incorruptible. At least he hopes he is.

Hammond is sitting behind a desk, perusing a file of papers with affected *gravitas*. He looks up as Henry walks in. Henry sees there are two other CIOs nearby.

Hammond looks down again, as if temporarily diverted by an insect he knows will not sting. But Henry stands his ground, facing him, and Hammond is forced to look up again.

'Do you want something?'

'I need to speak to you.'

Hammond sighs and drops his pen, sitting back and opening his arms in a gesture of attention. Henry looks around.

'Can we speak alone? It's just—' Henry flaps his hand in the direction of the other two. A nasty smile creases Hammond's chin as he gets up.

'Training room,' he says.

He leads Henry out and across to the opposite door on the corridor. Walking in, he switches on the strip lighting. Henry follows.

The nomenclature of the training room is something of a mystery – perhaps in the days when staffing levels weren't at rock bottom it made sense. Now its only purpose is as a bedroom for one of the night shift – one of the folding beds is a permanent fixture, pushed up against the wall. A small blackboard and a yellowed *Times Map of the World* grace the wall. On a small, two-shelf chipboard bookcase sit a number of training videos supplied by the service. These have titles like *Your Passport, Sir!* and *Firm but Fair: Immigration and You*. There are half a dozen copies of one called *Get in on the (Immigration) Act (1971)!*, which Henry has never been shown.

Henry closes the door and faces Hammond, who has his arms folded across his chest.

'I expect you've come to apologise for throwing that cup of coffee over me.'

'No,' says Henry.

'Then this conversation is over.'

He makes to leave, but Henry steps between him and the door.

'All right,' he says. 'I am sorry that I poured coffee on you. I apologise.'

Hammond puffs out his chest.

'And I'm sorry that I accidentally covered you in photocopier toner.'

Hammond sticks his tongue out, something which he often does when thinking.

'I accept. So this conversation is over.'

Again Henry has to stop him leaving.

'No. There's something else. I need—' Henry takes a deep breath '—your help.'

Henry has difficulty masking his distaste at such a confession. Hammond, too, is uncomfortable.

'I see. What is it?' he asks, grasping his cuffs in anticipation.

Henry gives him the story – the gook crook he saw in Soho, the lost file, the nicked stamps, the Heffer setup – without using Thorough's name, keeping his identity out of it, calling him 'this colleague' or 'this officer', holding back from going the whole way just yet, waiting to see how Hammond responds.

Hammond is perturbed, embarrassed at first at being the subject of anyone else's trust, then concerned. His eyes tighten and flicker. He stops holding his cuffs like a child so that he can quickly wrap his hands across his chest. As Henry winds up, he's looking down, his tongue rolling repeatedly across the front of his teeth.

'These are grave accusations,' he says. 'What I want to know is why you are telling me.'

'Because I'm next. After Heffer. It's going to be me with an envelope full of Triad passports falling out of my locker next with the Bitch—'

Hammond reacts.

'Sorry – with the Port Commissioner looking on. I'm telling you now because when it does happen you might believe me and see that I've been set up. I asked you,' Henry drops the intensity, 'because I knew that you'd be appalled that it could go on, that you wouldn't stand by and let this kind of abuse happen, especially if you knew that it was coming from—' Henry braces himself for the clincher '—one of our own.'

Even now, Henry has to stop a derisive laugh as he says it. But he sees that it's hit the spot. Hammond, the man of action, drops his arms to his side and pushes back his stooped shoulders.

'If any of this can be substantiated, if there is any truth in what you say, then it is clearly a case of the good name of the service being brought into disrepute. You would have done the right thing to bring it to my attention.'

A serious pause follows. They both know what it precedes. Hammond breaks it, his voice little louder than a whisper. 'You will, of course, be required to divulge the identity of the officer you think is involved.'

Henry nods, looks around, puffs his cheeks, raises his eyebrows, nods again, crosses his fingers . . . 'Ed Thorough,' he tells him.

Even before he's through the third syllable, Henry knows he's fucked. He sees it like a motorway signpost in the blink of panic that registers the name on Hammond's face as he takes a step back and reaches for the door handle.

'No . . . really, I refuse to listen to any more of this . . . this . . . to suggest that an officer of such seniority, integrity, of such integrity could be in any way . . . I won't sanction this . . . clearly your motives are . . . I'll be reporting this incident to the Commiss . . .'

Henry interrupts.

'It's too late. You already know. I'll tell Thorough you know.'

Hammond stops at the door.

'I'll deny it. I'll say I didn't believe you.'

'It's too late,' repeats Henry. 'You—'

Hammond bends forward, in some kind of pain, and puts the flat of both hands to his ears. 'No! There's nothing more to be said. No!'

And he stumbles out. Henry sits against the table in the training room and falls back with a groan, closing his eyes from the blinding strip light, waiting for his pulse to settle. Despite his predicament, he feels a certain satisfaction in the knowledge that all along he has been right about Hammond and the rest of them, that for mendacity and hypocrisy the lag hierarchy of Terminal C outdoes even his opinion of what they are capable of.

He leaves the training room and, ignoring a call from the control, heads to the tea room for a cup of instant coffee.

Another call goes out for IOs from the Tannoy.

Fuck it, thinks Henry.

There are a few IOs in the tea room, some winding down after casework shifts, others whose afternoon duties will start in a little over half an hour. All are absorbed in the television, which rumbles on ahead of them, having a laugh at a report on an afternoon news bulletin about a hunger strike at Thorpdown, an immigration detention centre in Hertfordshire. The TV shows a few detainees – Algerians and West Africans, by the look of them – who have managed to get up on the roof. They are shouting and waving sheets furnished with illegible messages.

'Go on,' says Dick Foster to the telly. 'Fall off.'

'Oi, look!' Some nameless sprog points at the screen. 'I fucking knocked that one off. There, him, the one throwing the slate off the roof. Yeah, he was one of mine. Fucking scrote.'

The voice of the TV reporter booms as someone turns up the volume.

'*. . . while other inmates have begun a hunger strike protest to highlight what they consider to be their unjust continuing detention . . .*'

A pantomimic groan from the assembled.

'Go on fucking hunger strike,' says Ken McCartney to the screen. 'Save us all a few bob.'

'*. . . immigration officials and police were able to remove protesters from the roof and have regained control of the affected wing. A delegation from the organisation Refugee Aid Forum were able to speak to inmates' representatives and explained their grievances during an impromptu press conference outside the Thorpdown complex this afternoon . . .*'

More groans and clicking of tongues as a woman, red-haired, flirting with middle age, appears in awkward close-up, microphones and miniature recorders shoved in her face. Miriam Cooper, no less, there to stir it up nicely.

'Cow,' says someone.

'Slag,' comments another.

Roger Thorne moves over from the coffee machine to the edge of the TV, looking down at the picture intently, stirring and sipping.

'*. . . spoken with these men,*' says Miriam. '*We believe that they have a genuine grievance and intend to continue to lobby against this barbaric practice of detaining against their will hundreds . . .*'

'Bollocks,' says Simon Topp, scraping the last of his microwave meal from the plastic tray.

'Shhhhh,' implores Roger. 'Turn it up,' he adds to the IO clutching the remote.

' . . . *who are not criminals, who have committed no crime, who have not been charged and who have come to this country for sanctuary precisely to escape this kind of state persecution* . . .'

'Fucking turn it off,' says Foster. 'I can't bear to look at the witch. I wonder who's paying for her to turn up there and tell a pack of bloody lies. Do you know how much she charges for an hour of her time?' he asks rhetorically, turning to a sprog. 'I'll tell you. Plenty. Fucking plenty. More than they pay us to protect this country!'

The report has finished. Roger hears Dick, shakes his head regretfully.

'What's the matter, Roger. Got the horn for Miriam, have you? Like a bit of rough, huh? I think you might be a little pale for her. Know what I mean?'

'Don't underestimate her. She's an intelligent woman.'

'Ooh, fuck me. I think it's love.'

'I'm not sure why we always need to be so confrontational.'

'Ah, come off it, will you? She's a fucking racketeer.'

A tart sting of coffee in his bladder forces Henry into the toilet next door.

The three urinals being free, he opts for the middle one. Pulling down his zip, he takes out his penis, holding it between finger and thumb. The urge to pee is there, but it lodges at the root of his member and seems reluctant to come forward. Henry sighs and bends his head back slightly, waiting for some action.

There is a sudden scratching of paper and an immediate flush from one of the cubicles. Henry looks across, pushes his backside out, waves his pecker, trying to engender a response in his frozen waterworks. But some valve stubbornly refuses to obey his brain, which is shrieking *please, please . . .*

The lock on the cubicle clicks back.

Ed Thorough emerges, *Daily Mail* rolled and tucked under his armpit. He moves to the basins behind Henry, who is praying for his prostate to snap into life. Thorough runs the water, but even that doesn't work for Henry, who feels as if there's an icicle been shoved down his urethra.

Thorough moves to a position directly behind Henry, pulls down hard once, twice on the rolling towel to dry his hands. Thorough moves alongside him.

The piss-free silence is giving Henry a headache.

'Like standing with your cock out, do you?'

Henry says nothing.

'Mind you, you might need the practice. Might be the only way you can make a living before too long.'

Henry's rage only tightens further the vice in his crotch. Still, he restrains his urge to respond, guesses that lashing out is not going to help him. He tries a different tack, still holding his dick in one hand. He doesn't want to know if Thorough's looking at it.

'Look, man, I don't know anything. I can forget about it. What do I care? I'm not bothered what you're doing. I don't even know what that is. Just lay off. I promise you. It goes no further.'

Thorough shakes his head. 'Naaaah. How can I trust you when you go and shoot your fucking mouth off to a fucking screw like Hammond. Of all people.'

Henry doesn't look at Thorough, but tightens his mouth.

'Come on,' says Thorough. 'That useless cunt?'

'He told you?'

'Course he fucking told me. Come down the embarks bar to find me, just now. You want to know why?'

'Why what?'

'You want to know why he came looking for me straight away?'

'Because he's a prick?'

'Well, he is that. But that's only part of the reason. The real reason is that I own him.'

Henry shakes his head. 'What does that mean?'

'He's so scared of me I could get him to come into work in a French maid's outfit. While he's mincing about, getting his rocks off giving sprogs a hard time, I've got him looking over his shoulder every second.'

'How come?'

Thorough snorts. 'You want to know? All right.' He leans against the wall between urinals. Henry sees him glance down at his member, still in his hand. Henry puts it away. Immediately the need to pee doubles in intensity. 'You probably don't remember, but Hammond went on relief to the coast to cover for another screw about four years go.'

Henry shakes his head.

'Anyway, he takes a little day trip on the ferry to the Hook of Holland or wherever the fuck it is the boats go from there. When he gets back, Her Majesty's Customs decide to give him the once-over. They say they're acting on a tip-off, but they were probably just doing it for a laugh. They hate each other down there, us and them. Goes way back. Something to do with an argument about parking spaces. So they have a rummage and – what do you know? – they find some . . . material.'

Henry scratches his nose. The urinals flush automatically.

'Nasty stuff. Kiddie stuff.'

Henry responds, a mixture of surprise and assent, though muted by his predicament.

'Oh, yeah,' Thorough goes on. 'Ralph's tastes are quite specific. Normally he'd be up before the beak. Customs want to prosecute. The Commissioner down there gets involved – him and Ralph had been IOs together. He has a word, gets the charges dropped with a warning.'

'So he got away with it?'

Thorough laughs once. 'Yes. And no.'

'Meaning?'

'Meaning that it's all there in his personnel file.'

'How?' Personnel files are kept in a locked safe in the inspector's offices.

Thorough shrugs. 'All you need is the combination and to know where to look. Interesting reading, some of them. Not yours, though: thinnest fucking file I ever saw. But that's how I found out about Ralph's little adventure. Of course, I let him know that I know, that it could be common knowledge if I chose. You saw what it did to him when you used my name.'

Thorough smiles sharply.

Henry takes a deep breath. 'So there's no way out for me?'

'No.'

'There's nothing I can do?'

Thorough looks puzzled. 'Like what?'

'Anything to make you lay off.'

'You mean . . . like a blow job? . . .'

The door to the gents opens. It's Ken McCartney, surprised to see anybody else in there.

'Hello, gentlemen,' he says, heading towards the cubicles.

'Ken,' says Thorough.

'Yes, Ed?'

'Toilet's closed.'

Ken laughs. 'What you on about?'

'Toilet's closed. Now just piss off. Quickly.'

'But I need to—'

'Use the ladies.'

Ken thinks for a second, recognises a quality in Thorough's eyes and shuffles out.

Thorough turns back to Henry and raises an eyebrow. 'Well?'

'I'm going to tell the Bitch,' Henry says.

Thorough blinks, shrugs. 'Go ahead, if you think it'll do you any good. You don't actually think he'll do anything?'

'Why wouldn't he believe it? It's the truth.'

'Yeahyeahyeah. I didn't say he wouldn't believe you. I said he's not going to do anything.'

'Why wouldn't he, if he thought it was the truth?'

Thorough looks down, laughs, shaking his head.

'Because he doesn't care about the fucking truth, son. How do you think he got as far as he did? By worrying about the truth and doing something about it? What truth? The truth that he's running a terminal full of drunks, Paki-bashers and crims? You think I'm the only one landing ratbags for money and fuck knows what else? You reckon you've stumbled over the crime of the century, but it's nothing. Nothing. The Bitch? When was the last time you saw him inspecting the control? Never. He's not interested. He doesn't want to know what goes on out there, getting his hands dirty. Just let the drunks and the Paki-bashers get on with it. That's how we all like it. But go and tell him, see how far it gets you.'

Thorough is strangely animated now, warming to his theme, pointing the rolled-up newspaper at Henry.

'So fucking what if I do a few favours? Nobody else is going to do me any. Stuck on the fucking maximum for fifteen years, not a sniff of promotion. What would you do, sprog, someone taps you on the shoulder and offers you two thousand for slipping a dodgy yellow a passport? You think it makes a difference if I say yes or no? You think I'm the only one—' He stops suddenly, in thought.

'You shouldn't have got in the way,' he adds, almost apologetically.

'I didn't mean to.'

'I figured that one out for myself. Not exactly Mr Knock-Off, are you?' says Ed, contemptuous again.

Ed looks around before continuing. 'Fucking hell. When I think of what I've put into this job. It's not like you can blame me taking an extra few quid. That's handy money to be making when you've been on the maximum for fifteen years and the promotion you should have had goes to some frigid bitch or some tosser with a degree in business management, like that twat Onions.'

'You set him up?'

Thorough shakes his head again.

'He was . . . stupid. He knew what was going on. When he came to me, I thought he was all set to blag me. But he needed some money, messy divorce or something. So he asked me if he could come in.'

He laughs quietly. 'Daft bastard didn't have it in him to stitch anybody else up, so he used his own stamp, with the fucking number showing. Only a matter of time before the Old Bill got involved . . . they were putting pressure on the Bitch to open it as a criminal matter after they found the yellow dead with Onions' cards. So the Bitch decided he needed to nip it in the bud. He needed someone he could trust to find out if Onions had any accomplices. And who did he choose? . . . Let's just say he chose the best man for the job. Me. Got to laugh, don'cha?'

Henry's not laughing

'By the way,' Thorough goes on. 'You'd better forget any idea of going to the pigs. First of all, you've got no evidence. No computer record, no file. And even if they did believe you, which is not very likely, these boys I'm dealing with – They're not nice people. Look what happened to that feller in Soho. And he was one of theirs.'

'You know who did that?'

'So do you. You let him in the country on Sunday, remember?'

Henry blinks, takes a deep breath, feels his knees about to buckle.

Thorough shakes his head, smiles. 'You *are* out of your depth, aren't you? Take the fall. That's my advice'

Henry's biting his lip now. 'So how much did Heffer know?'

'Fuck all.'

'So why him?'

'I've got to set somebody up. And I don't like the noisy little queer. No place for turdburglars like that in my Immigration Service.'

Ed laughs. 'Face it. You've got no way out. Not even for a blow job,' he adds.

Henry takes his chance to walk out, at least reserving himself that small vestige of pride. His bladder gnaws at him for relief. He rushes out towards the control and dives into the same public lav where Ed makes his passport collections at the top of the ramp that leads down to the Customs hall.

This time, the piss flows free. Henry sighs with satisfaction, looks up to the ceiling as gallons siphon out of him.

It's checkmate, he realises. He experienced a moment of epiphany as Thorough was speaking. He sees how right Ed was, about the Bitch, about the whole fucking service. They rap you on the knuckles for being five minutes late and think they're doing their job, while the rest of the time you are free to knock off and bang up as many people as you want with impunity, effectively unhindered by petty considerations of fairness and justice. They're don't care if you tell lies to chiefy to get someone refused or ignore a darky who's screaming for asylum because that's exactly what makes you a *bloody good* IO in this fucking madhouse. It's almost funny . . .

Checkmate, then, though it would be hard to just sit and wait for his fate. If only he had some proof, irrefutable proof.

Proof that he could take to the Bitch. But then, as Thorough suggested, if the Bitch knew anyway and wasn't prepared to do anything about it . . . then better to have something which proved *that*, which proved that the Bitch was at least complicit to that extent. If he could catch them in some kind of discreet hugger-mugger. Even then, Henry would have to be able to prove that he knew . . . he'd have to be able to . . .

The plan comes in a synaptic flash. Without even going over it in any detail, he realises that it's possible. But he also knows he has only one chance.

'It's a long shot,' he says out loud, shaking the last drops off.

A man wearing a dog collar at the next pissing station gives him a funny look, but Henry just smiles back.

At the first opportunity, Henry checks on the necessary information. Tomorrow is supposed to be his day off, but not coming in isn't an option.

He's in the duty office, checking the roster for tomorrow, which tells him what each IO is doing. By now, the sheet for Friday is awash with crossings out and corrections, where shifts have been swapped. Henry scans the page fast, looking for Thorough's name. Good, he's not off . . . Where, where? . . . There he is.

He's early forgery, due to start as the night shift clock off, at eight in the morning.

Next, he checks the sheet posted up on the notice board. This tells him if the big cheeses are present in the office and, if so, when. Again he's in luck. The Bitch is due in at about nine o'clock.

Tomorrow it is, then. Henry writes his own name at the bottom of the B shift, starting at 7.15 a.m.

The discovery that all the unwitting players are all in the right place at the right time gives Henry a momentary surge of elation, but he is brought clattering to earth by the reminder of how far-fetched his scheme really is. When it boils down to it, it relies entirely on luck. And ever since his first day working at Terminal C, Henry has never considered himself lucky.

chapter 5

long shot

Thursday

It's still Thursday.

Henry goes in through the clerical office, expecting it to be empty.

It is.

Henry looks at his watch.

Ten thirty.

Ten thirty *p.m.*

He's a little afraid, just cacking it a little bit. For a start, it could be that Thorough is still around, though the odds are against it. He considers bottling it and just leaving, but with dismissal and a possible prison sentence in the offing, it's as hard to do that as it is to carry on. He knows that he is taking a huge risk tonight, one probably out of all proportion with what he is going to gain. But the ball's in his court, and he has to make some kind of move to give his greater plan any kind of credible chance.

He has to try to lure Thorough into his snare, and he needs some bait. Simple as that.

He's dressed casually: jeans, trainers and a navy sweater, a rucksack dangling from his shoulder. He turns into the long corridor, dark now, and tries to walk as if this is exactly where he's supposed to be at this time of night. But the air-conditioners know what he's up to, hissing their displeasure at him.

As he approaches the door to the tea room, the first hurdle, he reminds himself of what he's already spent all day rehearsing. The light from the room spills out on to the corridor carpet. Henry hears the low boom of the TV from within.

He reaches the door and goes in.

There are two of them in there, Guldeep and Malcolm Cartwright, both staring at the TV, eating microwaved food off paper plates. Malcolm loves night shifts and swaps on to as many as possible, even when, as today, he's already worked a full shift. The office beds, small and smelly though they are, are still better than the reclined front seat of his Land Rover. Plus he gets his tuck for free, grabbing one of the meals-on-wheels-type concoctions served up in metal trays for the refugees in the pen. Most refugees eye them suspiciously before deciding not to risk eating them, but Malcolm is tucking into his Caribbean chicken or whatever it is. Whatever it is, they always call it chicken.

'What are you doing here?' he asks, a little suspiciously, Henry thinks.

Henry addresses the coffee machine and pops in twenty pence.

'Just popped in to pick something up. Something I left in my locker. I need it, that's all. I was just having a drink with a friend and he dropped me off here. It was the most convenient place for both of us, for him to drop me off and so I can take the Tube from here, you know? . . .'

He knows he's in danger of drawing attention to himself by going on in this witless fashion, but he's also aware of being very nervous. As it happens, nobody's paying any attention, not with Miriam Cooper on TV.

She's being questioned for a news programme, arguing with an abrasive interviewer.

'. . . *What I think your viewers need to understand is—*'

'*If I can just interr—*'

'. . . *What they must understand is . . .*'

'*I'd be grateful if you would just answer the question.*'

'*I'm trying to answer the . . .*'

'*Do you really . . .?*'

'*If you'll allow me to finish . . .*'

'*I'd like to hear your response to the question. Are you saying that there is no such thing as a bogus asylum claimant?*'

'*What I'm saying is—*'

'*Yes or No?*'

Miriam crosses her legs. Fatally, she pauses. '*No.*'

'*No, there's no such thing as a bogus asylum claimant?*'

'*Yes. That's right.*'

Guldeep sits forward, points at the screen. 'How?' he asks. 'How can she say that? How *can* she say that?'

'Shhhh,' says Malcolm.

'*Is there any such thing as an illegal alien?*'

'*Legally, yes. Morally, no.*'

'*What do you mean?*'

'*These people are not so-called illegals through any decision they have made. They are forced into the position of moving beyond the immigration rules by the fact that those very rules make their lives here intolerable. In one sense,*' Miriam rounds off, not disguising very well how pleased she is with herself, '*you could say that they live in fear from our government as well as their own.*'

Guldeep splutters.

'Amazing,' mutters Malcolm. 'Amazing.'

'You know what the greatest tragedy of all is?' says Guldeep. 'Twisting like that, she would have made a great head-hunter, innit? What a loss to the Immigration Service.'

But Miriam isn't finished.

'I should add that this view is not held only by those of us who assist refugees. I have alongside me at work someone who until recently was a senior officer with the Immigration Service at London Airport and who resigned in, well . . . quite frankly, who resigned in moral outrage at the treatment meted out by the Home Office to these genuine, I repeat genuine, asylum seekers.'

'Who's that?' asks Guldeep. 'Who do you think that is?'

'No idea,' says Malcolm over a mouthful of chicken surprise. 'Nobody from this Terminal, I don't think.'

Henry sneaks out and walks further down the corridor towards the main office.

He checks his watch. Ten forty. He's turned up at what he hopes is the time between the last scheduled flight arriving and those passengers having been cleared and last orders at the bar downstairs, where the rest of the night shift should be. Quickly entering the office, he sees that he's caught the right moment – nobody there. Even so, he knows that beyond the wall, there will be at least one chiefy in the watchhouse, wondering at the ill fate that has stalked him (or her) since they took the poisoned shilling of promotion. He has to be careful. He puts down his coffee and quickly slips into the forgery room, shutting the door behind him.

Inside, Henry switches on the Anglepoise, turning the base so that the light shines away to the corner, hopefully not betraying his presence.

He drops the rucksack off his shoulder and on to the floor. Crouching down, he pulls from it a crowbar and sets about attacking the top drawer of Thorough's desk, forcing the crow under the lip of the desktop and pushing down, gently increasing the pressure, pushing, pushing, pushing.

A crack and the drawer slackly rolls out. The sweat on Henry's brow and the back of his neck freezes. He listens, breathing hard through his nose. The air-conditioners shriek. Otherwise, nothing.

Henry grabs the Anglepoise by the base and shines it on the desk's contents. His worst fear proves groundless – it is not empty.

He rummages among the pens and pieces of paper, taking out some items and dropping them into his rucksack.

An envelope, with some money. About two hundred quid. He pockets it.

There are a couple of passports, one Chinese, one Korean, no endorsements inside them.

An address book.

Henry wonders if he has enough time to scrutinise the paper in the desk. He checks his watch. No. Besides which, he needs to make sure Thorough knows what he's done. There has to be no way he can miss it . . .

Henry pulls the drawer fully out of the desk and pours its entire contents into his rucksack. He leaves the empty drawer on the floor.

Outside, the office is still empty.

Henry's out and away, back down the corridor.

'See you,' he shouts at the tea room as he passes. He hears a grunt.

Henry reaches the door to the clerical office but doesn't make the turn. Instead he carries on, right down to the end of the corridor, right on to the Bitch's office.

He knocks on the door. No reply.

He goes in.

The Bitch's office is the prime site for kip on a night shift and is usually the property of the senior lag on duty. One of the folding beds is already down, a sleeping bag half-open on top. He checks the time again. He's got five minutes before they come back upstairs.

From his back pocket he pulls out an envelope, folded once. Inside it is a message, typed on a white piece of A4. It reads:

Mr Gascoigne,

Ed Thorough has been granting improper leave to enter to known criminals of Chinese nationality.

I have proof of this.

I will make myself known to you soon.

The envelope is sealed with Sellotape, to stop a curious night man from poking his nose in where it's not wanted. Henry moves around to the Bitch's side of the desk and mulls over where to put the letter. He decides against the in-tray. He has to be certain that the Bitch sees it, so he puts it right in the middle of the desk.

Then he glances across to the corner of the room, looking for the item that the whole plan relies on, without which there is no plan.

It's there.

The video camera's there, next to the pot plant.

Henry grabs the blank tape from the external pocket of his rucksack. Moving in behind the camera, he puts the tape in. He bends slightly to take a look through the viewfinder, adjusting the angle a few degrees to get the whole desk, both sides, in the frame.

He clicks the SLOW PLAY button. The longest tape he could get has a duration of ninety minutes, so by doubling the length he gives himself three hours of film time to get what he wants. Carefully he sets the timer, telling the camera to start filming at 8.57 a.m. the following morning. He wants the machine to be quietly rolling when the Bitch arrives, doesn't want him to hear the telltale click and whir of the recorder starting.

Everything depends on it.

*

By the time he gets back to the flat, Henry feels strange, a little giddy with what he's done. No going back now.

The skin on his face is sticky, the pores clogged with fear and the decay of Terminal C at night. He checks into the bathroom and splashes cold water against himself. He reaches for a towel and drags it down his eyes, nose and mouth. Pushing his wet hair back, he looks at himself in the mirrored door of the bathroom cabinet.

There, in his eyes, he sees something he hasn't seen since . . .

A spark.

Sees it and senses it.

Whatever the odds, the planning and execution of his counter-measure has reawakened adrenalin glands that have lain dormant for Christ knows how long.

He feels alive.

But how long would that last, when all he could rely on was one letter, a video camera and the Bitch?

That's all you got?

'That's what I got,' Henry says to his own reversal, which smiles back at him.

Friday

Henry sits in the staff room, facing the door of the forgery room, staring at it, biting his thumbnail. His other hand rests gently on his stamp, which sits in front of him.

Behind him, the room is abuzz with two pieces of news.

First, Dick Foster has got Sandgate. Jimmy Craddock has been usurped. That's the rumour. And the Terminal C rumour mill is infallible.

'Bastard,' mutters Sid Bennison.

'It's just talk. Maybe he hasn't got it,' says Dave Niblo.

'It would be that bastard's luck.'

'How did he pull it off?' Dave wants to know.

'He snuck in with a compassionate reason and personnel bought it.'

'What compassionate?'

'You remember when his wife broke her neck after the bungee rope snapped? Something to do with that.'

'I heard the police questioned him about that. Couldn't prove anything, though.'

'Did you ever meet her? Ugly bloody woman. She's the only known case of someone who looked better after hitting the ground face first from a bridge than she did before.'

'Sandgate,' says Dave Niblo. 'Shit. Jimmy'll be gutted. Who found out about it?'

'Someone on a night shift was looking through the Bitch's desk drawers, out of interest, saw the letter from personnel. Apparently there's a Gideon's Bible in there he nicked out of a Travel Lodge. Hardly very Christian.'

Shit, thinks Henry, praying that they didn't mess about with his letter.

'Dick Foster getting Sandgate,' says Simon, shaking his head. 'Dick fucking Foster.'

For Henry, too, the unfairness of a lowlife like Foster getting Sandgate ceases to be an abstraction and becomes a gnawing pain in his gut. For anybody else, he would feel envy, but an envy tinged by empathy with their pleasure. Even for Jimmy Craddock or Sid Bennison. But not for Foster.

The other item of news is for some a mere distraction, an amusement; for others it's bordering on the earth-shattering, something which has even shunted the atrocity of the Allports or the back-stabbing Dick Foster out of the conversation. It is from the old lags' corner that the strongest vibrations of *gravitas* emanate. Malcolm Cartwright, in particular, looks as if the sky has fallen in.

Roger Thorne has left the Immigration Service. But this,

unthinkable in itself, is only half the story. He's crossed over to the dark side and joined Miriam Cooper Associates as an adviser. He is the turncoat she gleefully announced last night.

'All our policies, all our procedures,' mutters Malcolm. 'The whole operation. In the hands of the enemy.'

But Henry's got more to worry about than Roger Thorne's recrimination for not being promoted. It's seven thirty and his future hangs by a thread.

•

Prrrrrrrrrrrrrrrrrrttttttrpppppppprrrrrrrrrt

Bang

Bang

Bang

Boom

For once, time flies by on the control, faces of all hues blurring into one shade of unremarkable humanity.

Gradually the seats in front of Henry begin to fill up with the normal blend of antipodean youth and Third World fetch-ups.

Today he feels he can stare back at the row of refusal shoes with a sense of justification.

You think you've got problems?

He's checking his watch every five minutes. At eight o'clock the thought shivers through him that Thorough should have arrived and discovered that his drawer has been broken into. Henry calculates that Ed's rage will have to be at least partly suppressed, that he'll have to be silent about what's been taken if not about what has happened.

Henry flashes another look behind him.

He's there. Thorough, standing on the steps leading up to the watchhouse, speaking to Sharon Barber, who's on duty. His face may be a little redder than usual, his mouth a little tighter, but he's not giving much away. Henry feels a depth charge in his gut, and he turns back, hunches himself over the desk and waits for the Bitch to come in.

Prrrrrrrrrrrrrrrrrrrrrrrrrrrrrrrrrrrrrrrrrrt

The usual morning onslaught continues. Henry's rolling everything that comes anywhere near him. He doesn't want to pick up a case this morning, whatever happens.

A Japanese flight is coming through. Henry gets a passenger from it. He is early twenties, hair dyed yellow, the colour of pus, ring through his nose. Wearing plastic drainpipes and a faggot's clubbing T-shirt. He hands his passport to Henry and starts fiddling with the earphones on his flash Walkman.

Henry takes a look at his document. The picture sourly amuses him, for it is a very different Akura Kamasura from the one who stands before him. Straight black hair, collar and tie, sober expression. This passport issued in London about three months ago, Japanese entry stamp from two weeks ago, coming back now.

'How long are you staying?' sighs Henry.

'I am student here.'

'Oh, yeah? Where's it say that on your passport?'

'I lost passport. This new passport.'

'Where do you study?'

'Keng'stong Chelsea Schoo' Art and Design.'

'Have you got proof of that?'

'Huh?'

'You don't speak very good English.'

Slope goes quiet.

'How long have you been in Britain?'

'I cu' for three mo' munf.'

Henry sighs again. 'No, how long have you already been here? When did you first come here?'

Slope contorts his face while he thinks about it. 'Five year,' he says.

Henry shakes his head. 'You really don't speak very good English.'

'I ha' cu' to do exam.'

'This is your first exam?'

'No. I fai' it befo'.'

'You're Japanese, you've failed an exam and you're still alive?'

Henry knows this could be a case and that it would be with the majority of his colleagues. He knows this ridiculous, yellow-haired geek is working in breach and probably hasn't seen the inside of a classroom since he gave his first blow job in the changing room of a King's Road boutique. He knows that, by everybody else's standards, this is a refusal, a stone-cold, bang-to-rights, duff as old boots knock-off standing in front of him.

But he doesn't care. I mean, he thinks, who *really* cares?

'Your lucky day,' he says and – *bangaboom* – stamps him through.

Henry's sleepless night begins to catch up with him as the queues start to dwindle. Again he glances at his watch. Twenty-past eight. He needs a coffee, thick and sweet, to prop up his eyelids.

Glancing backwards again, he sees an unwelcome sight – Sharon Barber approaching with intent. She intercepts a Jordanian on crutches and sends him the fifty yards back to the queue before standing in front of Henry's desk herself.

'I need you to come off the control and go into casework for an interview. They've overbooked and you're volunteering to do it.'

Henry groans. 'Why me?'

'Don't fucking start, lovey,' she says. 'Ralph Hammond's gone sick and I've got enough to worry about out here on my own. Just go in there and do your job, if you know what that is.'

This royally screws up Henry's plan. He doesn't want to be stuck in the interview room. He wants to be around when the Bitch gets in, to see him come in and then, when the Bitch sees the letter Henry's left him, he wants to be sure that he calls Thorough in to talk it over . . .

Oh, plus the fact that he doesn't want to do a fucking interview.

It gets worse.

It's a marriage interview, due to start at nine o'clock.

He takes the file reluctantly back to the main office to read it through. As he goes in, he notices the door to the forgery room firmly shut. Henry takes a seat at the opposite end of the office, facing it.

Jimmy Craddock is in, and from the blackness in his eyes he has obviously heard the bad news. The crutches have gone, but now he's sporting a plaster cast on his arm that Henry doesn't remember seeing before.

'That cheating Jock bastard,' he's muttering. 'Back-stabbing, cheating, lying little shit. He'd better not turn up today.'

Malcolm Cartwright has other matters on his mind. 'Can't understand it,' he's saying. 'Can't understand why he wouldn't let anybody know. Not even a clue. And then . . . Miriam Cooper, of all of them. Can't understand it.'

'He's best out of it,' says Jimmy. 'Best out of this shower of shit. Good luck to him. Back-stabbing *bar-sterd*. Best out of it, I tell you . . .'

There is an alarming bleakness in Jimmy's bearing. He's pissed, but more so than usual, pissed beyond his default state of raucous bonhomie and into an area more sinister and unpredictable.

'Well, he's gone and that's that,' says Sid Bennison.

'Not even a card. Not even a phone call,' continues Malcolm. He looks shattered after his night shift but is reluctant to return to the charms of the parked Land Rover.

And then Dick Foster walks into the room. Even by his standards, he's dressed down in grubby jeans and a tight T-shirt, emphasising his pigeon chest. Jimmy hisses.

'Hello, Richard. Rich-*ard*,' he says.

Foster grunts back at him.

'Have you heard the news?'

Foster looks suspicious.

'News?'

'About Roger, Rich-*ard*. About Roger Thorne.'

'What's he been saying?'

'He won't be saying much more. At least not to the likes of us.'

Foster turns to Malcolm, who avoids his eye-line. 'What's he fucking talking about?'

'He's gone and joined Miriam Cooper as an associate partner,' mutters Malcolm.

'That lazy cunt? He's from fucking Dundee. What d'you expect?'

'So what are you doing here, dressed like a tramp?' asks Jimmy, with more menace.

'Come to clear out my locker. My transfer to Sandgate's come through. I don't know. Maybe you heard.'

Sid Bennison coughs something. Foster, connoisseur of *Schadenfreude*, cannot resist giving vent to his pleasure.

'Well,' says Jimmy, getting up unsurely, 'we'd better start making arrangements for a party.'

'I'm not having any fucking party.'

'No,' says Jimmy, heading to the door. 'But we are. The minute you're gone.'

The buzz of antipathy between them for the moment before Jimmy leaves is enough to even drown out the air-conditioners.

Henry has never really understood just how violent the passions surrounding a transfer to Sandgate can be. Until this moment.

He glances at the time. One minute to nine. The camera is rolling.

Henry opens the interview file he's been given and begins to half-read it, keeping an eye on Thorough's door. It refers to an Egyptian national, Ali Nzaad el-Foussy.

He arrived six weeks earlier in the company of a Portuguese woman six years his senior, Maria Ferreira. He attempted to gain entry by presenting a forged Swedish passport in the identity of Norbert Huggerson. When this elaborate deception was uncovered, he gave his real name as that on the file and produced a valid Egyptian passport which did not contain the mandatory visa. He stated that he was married to Ms Ferreira and asked to apply for leave on that basis – that is, being the spouse of a citizen of the European Union. As it was a Sunday and resources were overstretched, he was granted temporary admission to his wife's address, as she lives and works in the UK. Today's date was set for their interview, designed to assess the credibility of the marriage.

In the meantime, the passenger's name has been referred to the Home Office, who have sent Terminal C a three-inch-thick file on him. He has, over the past four years, made nine unsuccessful attempts to gain a visa for the United Kingdom. These break down as follows: four visit visas (these were refused because in each case his sponsor, Mr Hoggar, is serving six to eight in Wandsworth Nick for fraud); three student visas (including one refusal pertaining to a stated intention to do a course in advanced motorcycling); one application to come to the United Kingdom as the sole representative of a new business (refused on the basis that his uncle's fruit stall was an unlikely candidate for inter-continental expansion); one failed attempt to get a refugee visa (which do exist), when it was noted that the passenger worked as a driver for the Ministry of the Interior.

After these, he had chosen to dispense with the visa formality and had turned up with his Swedish fake. It falls to Henry to ask him and his new spouse questions individually: how they met, what they do together, what colour toothbrushes they each use, etc., etc.

For real IOs, marriage interviews are the best chance to exercise the full range of their invasive powers. To assess whether or not a marriage is actually subsisting gives the right to probe into areas that Henry has no wish to be privy to. An IO can even recommend a home visit to such a couple, where a squad arrive unannounced to rummage around for proof of nuptial bliss. This practice is known as *mattress-sniffing*.

Henry closes the file and sighs. The clock on the wall tells him it's just after nine. The Bitch should be in now, should have seen the letter. The pawns in Henry's endgame might be about to move on to the right squares.

Sharon Barber comes in, huffing. She shouts across to Barry Venables, who is commiserating over the loss of Roger.

'Barry,' she interrupts him tersely. 'Have you seen Bob Gascoigne?'

Henry's ears prick up.

'What's that? Oh, Bob? Bob's going to be late. He called earlier and asked me to tell you. Sorry. There's a meeting at headquarters. Should be here about eleven.'

Fuck! Henry grimaces. Stay calm, he tells himself. Eleven, that still gives him nearly an hour of tape time. Once he sees that letter, he's bound to act on it straight away. Bound to . . . has to . . .

'*Henry Brinks*,' comes a voice over the Tannoy. '*Henry Brinks. Your nine o'clock interview is here.*'

As Henry gets up, the door to the forgery room snaps back,

almost ripped off its hinges by Thorough, who stands on the threshold, staring at Henry, mouth open.

Henry looks back at him. The thump of his heartbeat is making his fillings rattle, but he can see that he's managed to get to Thorough, that Ed is surprised by how far Henry is prepared to go. Christ, Henry is surprised at himself.

They stare it out. Like gunfighters. Thorough is the first to flinch, retreating back into his sanctuary. Henry heads to the interview rooms, walking tall.

'So, where did you meet?' Henry asks.

He is talking to Miss Ferreira, a Portuguese interpreter recycling the questions and answers. She is probably the ugliest woman Henry has ever seen in his life. The only symmetry in her face comes from the one giant eyebrow which stretches from ear to ear before swooping down each cheek to produce her bushy sideburns. Her nose appears to have been stung by a swarm of bees, or perhaps used as a hive. It might be an optical illusion, but he's sure that one of her eyes is half an inch lower than the other. However, it would be a simple matter to rest a spirit level on the natural escarpment of her prominent brow.

Miss Ferreira answers.

'We met in Cairo,' comes the second-hand reply.

Henry notes it down.

'Cairo. Right. What were you doing in Cairo?'

'I was taking my holiday.'

'Holiday in Cairo.' Henry raises an eyebrow. He once considered going to see the pyramids, but balked at the cost. 'How much did this holiday cost you?'

She shrugs. 'She don't remember,' says the interpreter.

'Well, how long was it for?'

'About a week. She don't really remember.'

'And what did the package include?'

'There was the flight both ways and all of the meals and hotel paid. It has four stars, the hotel.'

Henry makes a conservative estimate. A thousand pounds.

'So, who paid for your holiday?'

'I pay,' says Miss Ferreira, in English.

'She pay,' says the interpreter.

'Ask her what she does for a living,' Henry asks.

'Cleaner.'

'Full-time?'

'Part-time.'

'Part-time cleaner,' Henry repeats, writing it down.

Stephen H. Opuku, immigration consultant representing Mr and Mrs el-Foussy, shuffles in his chair. 'I feel,' he says, his West African accent strong, 'that it is my solemn duty to object to the line of questioning on which you are embarking with relation to my client in this manner.'

'Sorry?' says Henry, who has heard him perfectly well.

'I have said that I feel there is no justification for the enquiries you are putting as suggested in the questions you are posing to my client at this time. These questions are . . . unnatural.'

'Unnatural?'

'That is correct.'

'In what way unnatural?'

Stephen H. Opuku, immigration consultant, puts his hands together as if in prayer. 'It is my professional opinion that your interrogation of my client in this way constitutes a violation of her civil rights. And human rights also,' he tacks on for good measure.

Stephen H. Opuku is not, *per se* and *ipso facto* as he would no doubt put it, a lawyer. In order to set up in business as an immigration consultant, working on behalf of refugees and others with a 'matter' to be thrashed out, you apparently need only to be able to spell 'immigration' and 'consultant'. The rest just looks after itself.

'I see,' Henry says. 'The thing is, I have to ascertain the circumstances in which your clients met as part of the interview. I will note your objection. Otherwise, you may wish to take the matter up with the Security Council of the United Nations.'

Stephen H. Opuku nods and sits back. 'I have this very thing in mind,' he says.

Henry sighs and returns to Mrs el-Foussy. 'So how much do you earn as a cleaner? Part-time?'

'Fifty pound a week.'

'You get Housing Benefit?'

'Yes.'

Henry frowns. 'So, how long did it take you to save up for this holiday?'

'Don't remember.'

Henry glances at his watch, feeling suddenly very tired. He's been in here an hour, trying to think of questions to ask this gargoyle. Meanwhile, further down the corridor, he can almost hear the knives sharpening for him. The Bitch must be in by now.

'So where did you meet your husband?'

'At a bar.'

'What was it called?'

'The Pink Parrot.'

'And how did you meet?'

'He came over and brought me a drink and said that he wanted to get to know me.'

She smiles at the memory. Unfortunately this does nothing to improve her looks, as it serves only to reveal her assortment of yellow and black teeth and pushes out her lantern jaw further.

'Tell me,' asks Henry. 'How long was it before the question of marriage came up?'

She thinks for a moment. 'It was the next day that he mentioned it.'

'The following day?'

'The next day.'

'And how did the subject come up?'

'He said we should get married.'

'And you agreed?'

'Of course.'

'Why of course? Why so soon?'

'Because I love him.'

'You knew this after one day?'

'Oh, yes. He is so generous. Nobody ever bought me a drink before.'

'I bet,' Henry mutters.

This kind of case is pretty common. The holiday to Cairo was paid for by el-Foussy or possibly his dodgy sponsor over here. The meeting arranged, the marriage a foregone conclusion for which she will be paid, probably in a lump sum. A thousand quid, maybe. As a citizen of the European Union, she is exercising her treaty rights in bringing him to the UK. Effectively this means that there is nothing that the UK Immigration Service can do about it once he gets himself here, except pry into the colour of toothbrushes and generally put the wind up them.

Half-heartedly, he asks a few more questions before it's Mr el-Foussy's turn to bat.

'So, where did you meet?' Henry asks him, getting down to brass tacks after forty minutes of questions about his failed visa applications, punctuated by a number of Perry Mason-style objections from Stephen H. Opuku, immigration consultant.

He is tall, well groomed, handsome.

'In Cairo. A bar called the Pink Parrot,' says the interpreter, a different one. One who speaks Arabic.

'This was the first time you had met?'

'*Na-am.*'

'Yes.'

'Was it in any way an arranged meeting?'

'*La.*'

'No.'

'May I ask how you communicate at home? What language do you speak to each other?'

'We have our own language.'

'Your own language? How does that work exactly?'

El-Foussy scratches his nose and replies. 'You know, hand signals,' is the translation.

Henry suppresses a smile before the next question. 'What exactly was it that drew you to her exactly?'

Mr el-Foussy listens to the questions. He frowns, looks at the interpreter and speaks.

'He does not understand the question. I repeat it?'

'Yes, but . . . put it to him this way. What made him go over to her and ask her to have a drink?'

El-Foussy listens to the question again, showing that he understands it this time. Even so, he does not answer immediately, thinking it over.

Henry puts down his pen and stretches back, looking at him, eyebrows raised.

El-Foussy smiles and utters a few glottal stops. 'I thought that she had a nice personality.'

And el-Foussy laughs. The interpreter tries not to. Henry cannot help but smirk back at him. Stephen H. Opuku, immigration consultant, doesn't have a clue what is going on.

'As you can clearly see, my clients are very much in love. And here,' he goes on, producing a plastic bag stuffed full, 'I submit this variety of supporting documentation in respect of their application, incorporating video recordings of the marriage service and several photographs of the most happy couple.'

'Great,' says Henry. 'I'll have a look through and get back to you as soon as possible.'

'There is one other point which the Home Office may wish to be taken into consideration of the final judgement.'

'Which is?' asks Henry.

'It is that my client's wife is heavy with child.'

El-Foussy is looking a little pained, sad-eyed at the memory of a shameful necessity. Henry nods, eyes widening in awe. He's come across people who've fled certain death, people who've walked for hundreds of miles across desert in the hope of freedom, people who've hidden knee to chin in lorries for weeks, sustained by nothing but water passed through a straw from outside. He's even once seen a man who stowed away in the hold of an aircraft and came within an ace of freezing to death.

But he's never met anyone prepared to go as far as el-Foussy to get into Britain.

He comes out of the interview at 11.28. In the office, Sharon Barber is on the phone.

'Is he there yet?' she asks.

She gets a response in the negative.

'Well, has he called in? I'm supposed to see him this morning.'

She listens for a few seconds more before slamming the receiver down.

'Right,' she says to the IOs heading out of the door to meet another flight. 'I'm in a terrible fucking mood, so I want something to refuse. Understood?'

Henry assumes the Bitch isn't there yet. His tape has been

running for over two hours. Two hours film of an empty desk. It might win him the Turner Prize, but it's not going to save his bacon.

He sits down and empties the plastic bag on to the table. Out drops an assortment of letters, photos and other bits and pieces. The video falls out last with a clunk. It's been labelled OUR WEDDING – MADEIRA 1998 with a few hearts drawn on for decoration, a nice attention to detail. Henry's seen enough of these to know exactly what it will be like: rent-a-crowd, painted smiles, camera-shy Svengali figures lurking at the edges, giving hand signals and surreptitious instruction. Then the reception in some tatty church hall, toasting with plastic cups, the first dance to 'Simply the Best' (always, *always* Tina Turner), the cameraman's faculty stretched as he tries to make fifteen people look like a hundred.

But hell, these are just hoops you go through. They're married, they've got a certificate to prove it and that's that. It's a loophole, but this is one dodge which has no parameters of nationality or wealth. Marriages of convenience prove just as convenient for American superbitches who decide that they like living in Chelsea as for poor South Americans and Africans. The superbitches just pay more and never have to suffer the indignity of displaying their bloodied sheets to the village elders.

Besides which, if Henry refuses el-Foussy, he's just going to turn around and play his joker.

Henry glances through the photos. Most of them have been taken in her council flat by a third party, with the couple hugging or shoving spoonfuls of processed food into each other's mouths. He starts to put them back into the bag.

Past the door of the office, he snatches a sight of the Bitch walking past. He's carrying a suitcase and wearing a raincoat, so he must have just arrived.

It's twenty-two minutes to twelve. There's still time. But not much.

From the other door, Jimmy Craddock walks in, back from a trip to the bacon van via the departures bar. Pork grease, pints of bitter and whisky chasers are all writ large around his half-closed eyes. He stumbles across the room and sits down next to a dozing Malcolm Cartwright, who offers him a melancholy smile. Jimmy slumps himself forward and looks along the desk to where Dick Foster is sitting, chomping on a bag of Scampi Fries, a pile of yellowing papers in front of him, most of which he's dropping into a wastepaper bin at his feet.

'I'm not having it,' gurgles Jimmy. 'Not fucking having it. Do you hear me?'

Everybody does, but pretends not to.

The Tannoy is the first to speak. '*Sharon Barber to the Port Commissioner's office, please. Sharon Barber to Bob Gascoigne's office.*'

Oh, no! A pulse of frustration darts up Henry's back and down his arms. Sharon comes back in, flexing her freshly painted lips, bobbing on her high heels.

By his calculation, there are another sixteen minutes on the small plastic spools of destiny.

Around him, Henry senses an empathetic increase in tension, all deriving from the corner where Jimmy Craddock and Dick Foster are sitting, separated only by Malcolm, who's looking down at his hands.

'Do you fucking hear me?' repeats Jimmy, shouting now at Foster, his face twisted into a gargoyle expression. 'Do you hear me, you slag? I'm not having it.'

Foster's forehead has turned crimson. 'So you're not having it? Big deal. So fucking what?'

Jimmy crashes his plaster cast on the desk. 'You . . .' he whispers now, frightening. 'You . . . caaarrrrnnnt.'

A pause follows, electric.

'You . . . dirty farking carrrnnnnnt.'

'Shut your mouth, you drunken twat.'

Malcolm suddenly plucks up the courage to say what's been on his mind. 'You should have stood aside, Dick. You should have stood aside and let Jimmy take Sandgate. It was his transfer, not yours. You compromise the entire operation with that kind of behaviour. You had no right going over his head.'

'I had every fucking right. What did that prick ever do for me? Fuck all, like all the fucking rest o' ya'. I owe him nothing. And the same goes for your bumchum Roger Thorne. Everybody knows what a work-shy arselicker he was, prancing around, granting indefinite leave to his wife's family on the sly.'

Malcolm is outraged. 'That is abso . . . that's slanderous, libel. Disgusting. You have no idea what Roger has done for this terminal . . .'

'I know what I see with my own eyes. I knew that as soon as someone else gets Sandgate, he spits out his fucking dummy and pisses off. Don't kid yourself, he was trying to get Sandgate just the same, spinning you all a line about standing aside. When I was down at personnel yesterday, he was there, kneeling on the carpet, begging them to let him go, crying like a baby when they said no. So don't give me that bollocks. And as for this drunken shite . . .'

Jimmy tries to stand up at this reference. He is hunched forward like an ape, clenched fists resting on the desk before him. The already burst veins on his face are ready to re-erupt.

'Well, I've got fucking news for you, sunshine. You're not getting Sandgate either, you . . . caarrrnnnttt . . .'

'Oh, aye? What are you going to do about it, apart from filling your incontinence pants?' taunts Foster.

Jimmy reverts to the harsh whisper, hissing slowly: 'I . . . am . . . going . . . to . . . fucking . . . kill . . . you.'

Dick Foster gets out of his chair but is already too late. Jimmy, a vicious man-beast now, has scrambled on to the desk and thrown himself directly at Dick, hands outstretched for his throat. Foster tries a sideways swerve, but Jimmy is able to ring neck and shoulder with his good arm and haul him back. Jimmy slides off the table and lands with a thud, still clinging to Foster and, springing up, is able to push him back on to the desk, his plastered forearm pushing down hard on his throat, his free hand grabbing the bundle of Dick's testicles and crushing hard. A fountain of half-masticated Scampi Fries spurts forth.

Foster pinned beneath him, Jimmy moves in, teeth bared like a giant cat. Their faces are a beermat-width apart.

'Ready?' snarls Jimmy, absolutely fucking barmy.

Foster gurgles.

'Are you ready?' Jimmy says with an evil quarter-turn of the head.

Foster motions that he is not.

'Ready?'

'Ngggrrrr!'

'READY?'

'Nggraaaarrarrrrrggghhh!'

Jimmy plunges head first and lands hard on Foster's face with his own in a deranged, brutal French kiss.

Beneath him, Foster twists, wriggles, utters a low moan.

A couple of others, Dave Niblo and Simon Topp, make half-hearted attempts to get Jimmy off. When he does come up for air, he looks rabid, his bloodshot eyes tight, like an animal's in the glare of a headlight, his mouth a burst of blackberry.

Foster's hands go straight up to his face as he slides from the desk on to his knees. 'Whorrya done? Whorrya done?' he wails.

Jimmy totters back and, looking down, spits out the half of Dick's nose he has just bitten off.

Henry sits, open-mouthed, looking on. *Perhaps now,* he thinks, *perhaps now I have seen it all.*

Jimmy is dragged away, somewhere off the premises.

Unaided, Foster picks himself up and staggers out, towards the control and the Port Medical Inspector's office. Seconds later, from the same door, mad Sandy Reynolds comes in.

'I just saw Dick Foster wi' his face covered in blood. What the hell's been going on?'

Someone tells him the bare bones.

'What? You're kidding?' He puffs out his cheeks and emits a small snigger. 'Christ, that's one for the books. Why'd he do it? No, don't tell me. Jimmy must 'a had a reason. Anyway, never liked Foster. Serves that Jambo bastard right.'

This, Henry deduces, is a reference to Scottish football and, as such, not intended for general comprehension.

The consensus is that this knocks the Allports débâcle into a cocked hat. Roger Thorne's spectacular turncoat act is forgotten. IOs scatter to pass on the news to those unfortunate enough not to have witnessed it. One sprog bursts out into the corridor without looking and collides with Sharon Barber.

'Look where you're going, shithead,' she snaps, not best pleased. She's red in the face, fanning her cheeks. But she's out of the Bitch's office, with about eight minutes to go. It could just be enough, just. If he calls him in now.

But the Tannoy rests silent. Time shuffles busily around the clock face, the precious tape passing from roller to roller on the cassette, valueless.

Henry sits, legs crossed tight, tapping the desk.

'Please, please, please,' he hums. 'Please.'

'Would Ed Thorough go to the Port Commissioner's office. Ed Thorough to Bob Gascoigne's office.'

The time? Eleven fifty. Seven minutes of tape time left. If it takes a minute to walk to the office, that should be enough. Yes, about a minute to the Bitch's office from the forgery room.

But the forgery room door doesn't open. He must have heard the call, must have.

Henry gets up, time accelerating around him.

He bursts into the forgery room.

Nobody there.

He sees the drawer, his handiwork clear, sticking out like a tongue.

Quickly, he's in the corridor, looks left, right, has to choose. He goes right, towards the Bitch's office. Maybe Ed's already on his way, maybe Henry will catch a glimpse of him going in.

He runs fast down the corridor and headlong into Thorough, who's just come in from outside.

'You,' says Thorough.

'Yeah,' gasps Henry, leaning forward, hands on knees. 'There was . . . a call . . . The Bitch wants to see you.'

'You touch my fucking drawer?'

Henry waves his hands to signify the negative. 'Me? No. No way. It's just that Gascoigne wants to see you.'

'Yes . . . And?'

'I just wanted to make sure?'

'Of what?'

'Just to say that you should hurry. He doesn't like to be kept waiting. I just wanted to let you know that he was looking for you. In case it's important. I wanted to help you out, you know?'

Thorough eyes him coldly.

'Don't think I'm going to change my mind,' he says and heads down towards the Bitch's door. Henry goes into the tea room but sneaks back out to a spot where he can see down the corridor.

Thorough knocks once and goes in.

Henry doesn't dare look at his watch as he stares at the door. He is vaguely aware of his name being called over the Tannoy, barely audible over the sound of his own pulse in his head.

'Henry Burr-inks, Henry Brinks to the casework office immediately.' It's Rex Gibbons, Chief Immigration Officer.

In a large glass booth in the corner of the casework office, American police chief style, Gibbons is seated, waiting for him.

'Brinks,' he says with a cough and a big twitch, one that rocks his head back and pushes a lock of hair into his eyes.

'You wanted to see me?'

'That's what I said, wasn't it?'

'That's what you said.'

'It's report time, as you know. I think it's only fair we should have a chat before I submit what I think of you.'

'Whatever.' He eases himself into the chair opposite.

'Brinks, Brinks, Brinks,' sighs Gibbons with a shake of the head. 'You might take some time to think how you're going to improve your performance.'

Henry blinks slowly.

Gibbons picks up a beige folder, quite possibly the same one the Bitch had the other day. His personnel file. Opening it, Gibbons snorts hard, an act that he has to follow by coughing back up the mucus he has forced down the back of his throat.

'You're not refusing enough people,' he says, slapping the file shut.

Henry shuffles.

'You need to be refusing more people. You are well below the average for the port and you're even lower than the average for my team of IOs.'

'I don't see that many people to refuse.'

'You see the same as everybody else.'

'Maybe they refuse too many.'

'You are paid to refuse people. You're not refusing people, you're not doing your job.'

'But—'

'But what?'

'Maybe there's no reason to refuse them.'

'Who?'

'The people that I'm not refusing. Maybe I'm not refusing them because there's no reason why they should be refused.'

'You find a reason.'

'What reason?'

Gibbons sighs through his teeth. 'If they are refusals, there's always a reason.'

Henry's brow furrows. Listening to this shit makes him feel bloody-minded. And as things are standing, he doesn't have a lot to lose.

'So you want me to refuse passengers that I don't think should be refused?'

Gibbons clicks his tongue and drops Henry's personnel file on the desk between them. 'What you think doesn't matter. Don't think, sonny Jim, just get those refusal numbers up.'

'But why?'

'Because I tell you. *Be-cause* it's your job.'

'No. I mean, what for? What do you want me to refuse them for?'

'I want you to refuse them so that you get your number of refusals up.'

'No, I understand that. What I mean is, what do you want me to tell these people that they are refused for?'

'Don't give me any more of your lip, boy. There's an Act full of reasons, although I don't suppose that you've ever taken the time to read it . . .'

Henry pauses again.

'So, what you are saying to me is that I should refuse people on an arbitrary basis?'

'You can use any basis you like. Just send 'em back. Just get out there, stop the first passenger you see, sit them down, I don't care who they are, just sit them down and knock them off. That's what the Act is for. The Act is your friend, it will help you to refuse as many people as you want. Then we'll all be happy.'

'What if I refuse?'

Gibbons threatens to snort himself through the ceiling. 'Eh?'

'What if *I* refused to refuse more people?'

Gibbons leans forward. 'Then I'll mark you down.'

A stand-off. Marking down means a cut in pay.

'Whatever happened to firm but fair?' asks Henry.

'I don't care about that. What I care about is the number of people you're refusing, which, I repeat, is too low. You're showing everybody else up. Look at this file, man. There's nothing in it. You've been in the service for five years and you've not had one complaint against you.'

'And?'

'That shows me that you're not doing your job, getting stuck in.'

'You want me to get complaints from the public?'

'If you're not getting complaints,' says Gibbons, reciting an axiom, 'you're not doing your job properly.'

'You want me to actively go out there and try to get the public to complain about me?'

'I want you to do your job. You're showing everybody else up,' he repeats.

'How?'

'What?'

'How am I showing everybody else up?' Henry laughs sarcastically.

'Because you're dragging down the average. Paul Speerpoint doesn't refuse all those people every year just to see the likes of you drag down the average. Now, there's an example of a bloody good IO. You could learn a thing or two from the likes of him.'

Pause. Henry's anger, his anger at Thorough, at Hammond, at the whole fucking lot of them, is making him shake. 'Have you ever stopped to think,' he asks, 'how utterly ridiculous this all is? Do you think anyone on the outside would believe this conversation that you and I have just had?'

Gibbons catches a snort and forces it back out through his nose. He takes off his glasses, folds them and places them on the desk.

'Take a look out on that control, sonny. Take a look out there, look at the scum that drifts in and tell me everything's all right with the world. Tell me we've got nothing to defend ourselves from. Tell me it's not a bloody siege twenty-four hours a day, seven days a week.'

Henry shakes his head. 'I don't want to be part of your paranoid fantasies.'

To Henry's surprise, Gibbons refrains from going ballistic. He just clicks his tongue in resignation, shakes his head with stylised regret. 'It's no skin off my nose, son.'

Henry can't hide his mystification at such a phlegmatic response.

'I've been keeping it quiet, but you might as well know. This is my last day,' explains Gibbons. 'I'm retiring. So none of your smart-arse talk can bother me. But I'll say this. If you started to do your job and *think* like an IO, it might show everybody else which side you're on. People here don't like to see the service talked down. People like you corrupt it, corrupt what we do. You help the scum out there, not with what you do, because you don't do anything, but with what you say, what you think.'

'I corrupt it?' repeats Henry, aghast. 'You're telling me *I* corrupt it? You want to know how funny that is. You really do.' Standing up, he feels like being sick. 'Is that it?' he asks.

'That's it.'

Henry makes to leave, mouth open.

'Oh, by the way,' says Gibbons.

Henry scratches his neck. 'Er . . . yeah.'

'They're having . . . I'm having a little get-together down in the tea room in a few minutes. Sandwiches, a few cakes, just to say goodbye, you know . . . If you wanted to? . . .'

'Thanks, but I can't. I've got to . . . you know, go.'

'Fine.'

Henry can tell that Gibbons is relieved, that the invitation was no more than a formality. 'Well, goodbye,' says Henry.

'We'll be seeing each other again,' Gibbons replies.

'Will we?'

Gibbons smiles, showing a mouthful of metal. 'Yes, well, I'm not giving away any secrets by telling you this,' he says, puffing out his chest. The fact is that I've been offered a job by Royal Sheikh Airlines. As a consultant . . . I'll be doing a variety of work, but I think they want me to represent them in carriers' liability cases, try to get them off a few charges. I start on Saturday.' He winks, amused.

You fucking hypocrite, thinks Henry. 'Oh, right,' he says, and leaves.

It's some time after midnight.

Henry is sitting on the floor of his living room, facing the television. Inside the video player tucked beneath it the tape from the Bitch's office has finished rewinding.

He has sneaked in again, like last night, and reclaimed it from the camera. His main worry was that it wouldn't be there, but that proved unfounded. This time he had made no attempt to disguise his action. He went in, got the tape and got out.

Henry picks up the remote and points it at the player.

PLAY

There it is, the picture he set through the viewfinder, the Bitch's desk in wide angle and glorious colour. And there, on the desk, clearly visible, is the letter.

He remembers that the Bitch was two hours late for work, so he wants to jump to approximately that time.

STOP

FFD

Two hours of playing time are measured by the on-screen gauge.

STOP

PLAY

The same shot flashes back up. Still no sign of the bastard.

FFD

The Bitch's office is disturbed by two fat horizontal lines as Henry speeds up the tape. He concentrates on the door handle in the background, looking for the first sign of movement.

There!

At high speed, the Bitch waddles into his office and looks around like a villain in a silent movie.

REW

The Bitch stops and walks backwards out of the office at high speed, the door closing magically behind him.

STOP

PLAY

After about three seconds, the handle rattles and the Bitch enters again, this time at normal speed. He's wearing the raincoat and carrying the briefcase that Henry recognises from the morning.

Henry sits, not breathing, still afraid that the Bitch sees the giveaway red light or detects the sound of the camera with his reptilian hearing. But no, he comes in and moves towards the desk.

Henry watches, willing the two-dimensional figure, the collection of pixels and artificial light, to see the letter on the desk.

But the Bitch, even in simulation, is doomed to defy him. His attention caught by something beyond the giant window of his office, he places his briefcase on the desk and pushes it, sending the letter towards its edge, where it teeters for a second before dropping to the floor below, out of the Bitch's sight.

Henry grabs at the back of his neck in horror. He pulls his legs to his body and rocks forward, chewing a thumbnail. 'Come on,' he says to the screen. 'Come on, baby, pick up the letter, pick it up.'

But the Bitch can't see the letter. Instead he hangs up his coat and sits behind the desk, picking up the phone and dialling out.

'*Hello, Marjorie, it's me . . . I took the car in . . . Why no. They think I was at a meeting . . . Listen, the man said it needed a new filter . . .*'

Henry's patience corrodes quickly. He wants to cut to the chase.

STOP

Blue screen.

FFD

He lets the tape run until it has about ten minutes to go.

STOP

PLAY

The letter is still lying on the floor, refusing to draw attention to itself. The Bitch is seated again, jacket off now, looking pensive, even a little melancholy. Henry can't see for the desk, but he appears to be brushing some crumbs off his lap. The blue plastic bag which must have had his sandwiches in it is on the desk, taken out of the briefcase, which is open now.

The Bitch just sits there, just sits with a glum look on his face while the seconds fall away, drop off the end of the world.

'Come on, baby,' says Henry, clapping his hands in encouragement. 'Come to mama. Pick up the letter.'

The Bitch stirs, breathing once, twice, hard through the nose. He plants both hands on the desk and rises.

'That's it, Bitchy. That's it. Now just look down. C'mon Bitchy, you can do it . . .'

The Bitch moves out from behind the desk, moves out to the side where the letter is . . .

'That's it, Bitchy . . . Come on . . .'

. . . and looks down at the letter as he treads on it.

'Yes!' whoops Henry.

The Bitch picks up the letter.

'Yes,' says Henry. 'It's addressed to you. Now open the fucker . . .'

The Bitch tears it open.

'That's good. Read it. You can read, can't you, Bitchy? Oh, hurry up, for Christ's sake. You don't need to read it twice. Yes, yes, go on, do something, you fat git!'

The Bitch moves, though without great urgency, and picks up the phone.

'*Put a call out for Ed Thorough to come to my office.*'

'Good, good,' says Henry, leaning forward as far as he can now, tight in the foetal position.

The Bitch puts the plastic bag into his briefcase, which he closes and moves off the desk. He puts his jacket back on and takes a look at himself in the mirror on the back of the door. Peering forward to get a closer look, he takes the handkerchief from his breast pocket and dabs his forehead with it.

'Bit nervous, are we?' says Henry, his own bowels knotted with stress.

Time elapses, maybe two minutes, three. Henry knows he is giving it everything offstage, running the corridor like an idiot, cajoling Thorough towards his rendezvous. Meanwhile, the Bitch sits, rereading Henry's letter. There can't be much time left.

There is a knock and the door opens.

Ed enters.

The Bitch looks up and gestures for him to take the letter.

Thorough sits and reaches forward to take it. He stretches a leg and plants a booted foot on the Bitch's desk, who doesn't seem to mind.

Ed reads the letter.

The Bitch gets up.

'*I think . . .*' he begins.

'Yeah,' says Henry. 'Yeah? Yeah?'

'*It seems to me . . .*'

'YES? YES?'

'*. . . that we might have to—*'

And the video player clicks and the tape starts to rewind automatically and the screen goes blue and Henry's head drops on to his knee and he sobs at the cruelty of it, the cold fucking injustice of it.

With a groan, he lifts his head and rubs away an embryonic tear.

'That's it,' he says. His last gamble almost paid off, but now he will have incurred Ed's wrath even more and has nothing to show for it. He's sure that a few minutes more and he would have got what he wanted, there was something about Thorough's bearing in the Bitch's office that spoke volumes about their relationship. But by tomorrow, probably already, the inside of Henry's locker will look like the Shanghai passport office. He could always go back tonight and check on it, but Thorough might even be waiting for him, and if the evidence against him isn't going to come to light tomorrow, it'll be the day after or the day after that. All Henry can do is wait.

Besides which, he doesn't even have the energy to get up off the living room floor. So he sits, staring at the blue screen, wondering what the sentence is for facilitating a murderer. Three years? Five?

Chocolate stirs on the sofa behind him and jumps down on to his lap.

'What'll happen to Chocolate, eh?' Henry says, tickling her under the chin. 'What'll happen when they come for me?'

Hearing himself putting it like that, Henry's grip around the cat's neck involuntarily tightens. Chocolate yelps and digs a claw into Henry's thigh and he in turn throws her off him.

She lands on the video remote and stops the rewind.

PLAY says the blue screen. A moment later, the view of the Bitch's office is restored.

Henry reaches across for the remote, but the cat's kicked it just out of reach. Ready to stretch further for it, his eye is caught by a repetitive motion from the screen. He blinks, double-takes, but no, he was right the first time.

He leaves the remote where it is and stares at the box, goggle-eyed.

'Lord be praised,' he says. 'I am saved.'

He hears a sound in the corridor.

A footstep.

Another, nearer.

Christ! It's Thorough. Or Xiao! They've come for me!

He hits the PAUSE button. His jubilation freezes like liquid nitrogen.

Rising, Henry throws himself over the back of the sofa and moves behind the door. The footstep falls again, on a quietly creaking floorboard. Henry can deduce exactly where he is, only two steps from the door to the living room. All he has for a weapon is the remote. If his attacker has a knife, one well-aimed blow to the wrist might be enough to knock it out . . .

One more step. Then, carefully, gently, another.

The door to the living room slowly swings open. Through the gap between the hinges, Henry sees a figure move across the threshold. He lifts the remote above his head, ready to come down with it, take his one chance . . .

Across the room, he sees Chocolate stop licking herself and look up at the hidden figure and then nonchalantly skip towards it. His own pet prepared to sacrifice itself . . . The man behind the door swoops to meet her, ready to silence her purrs with a flash of his razor-sharp blade.

Catching a sight of a hand, Henry lunges.

'Here, kitty, kitty, kitty,' says a voice.

Henry screams.

Chocolate scarpers.

Jerome screams. 'What the fuck?'

Henry gasps. 'Jesus Christ, Jerome. I thought you'd come to kill me. What you doing, sneaking down the bloody corridor like that?'

Jerome pouts, rolls his eyes. 'Well, that's gratitude for you,' he says. 'I thought you might be asleep. I didn't want to wake you up.'

Henry lets out a lungful of relief.

'Anyway, as you're up,' continues Jerome. 'You can give me a hand with this.'

He lifts a brown paper bag, bearing the telltale sweat marks of a takeaway Chinese.

'And here,' adds Jerome, rummaging in a holdall bearing the name of his employers. 'This might help to calm you down.' He produces two miniatures of Courvoisier and chucks them at Henry.

'Cheers.'

Looking around, Jerome catches sight of the TV screen, still showing the frozen image from the Bitch's office. He double-takes, makes a face of lewd amusement.

'No doubt I'm showing my ignorance,' he says, 'but that doesn't look much like *Guns in the Afternoon* to me.'

Xiao stands in the queue, feeling self-conscious, uncomfortable in his ill-fitting suit, although he has to admit that by wearing it he fits in. He senses that the others in the group, all engineers from Nanjing, are afraid of him, afraid of this stranger who has suddenly, without explanation, replaced one of their number halfway through their fact-finding tour of British and American factories. But Xiao knows their fear will work to his benefit. One thing he likes about his compatriots: they always know how to keep their mouths shut.

As he shuffles forward, he feels no regret about leaving London. In his short time there he was aware of it as a tired place, where every angle was already covered, every corner taken, every space filled. He wanted more room . . .

So he wasn't unhappy when they told him he would have to leave. They didn't judge him for the killing he had committed. They understood the code and his adherence to it. But still he had to go; the situation was too dangerous for him to stay. He had brought more attention to their operation than they had wanted. He accepted their decision.

He reaches the front of the queue at the boarding gate and hands over his boarding card and the brown official passport that had belonged to the engineer so unfortunately hit by a motorcycle courier during a sightseeing trip to Covent Garden, the brown official passport now bearing Xiao's own photograph and containing the ultimate prize. An American visa.

The stewardess takes his documents and taps a keyboard in front of her. Above her head, a neon sign advertises flight number 189 and its destination.

She opens the passport and looks at the photograph, then checks for the visa.

'Thank you, Mr Zhu,' she says, handing them back. 'Hope you like Chicago. Have a good trip.'

For the second time in his life, Xiao boards an aeroplane.

chapter 6

firm but fair

Saturday

Henry doesn't go in dressed for work. He was due to start at seven o'clock, Right now, he's five hours late.

It's a good feeling – immunity. Immunity from the petty punishments, insulation from the system. Immunity from care.

He doesn't bother with the main office, not wishing to alert Thorough to his arrival. Not that Thorough matters. He's been leapfrogged. He's out of the equation.

Instead, he gets a coffee in the tea room. My last one, he wonders as the frothy top is gobbed out by the machine.

He passes the CIOs' office. Two of them in there, Barry Venables and Jamie Vedhara, are talking about Hammond.

'Amazing,' one says.

'I know,' agrees the other. 'Never taken a sick day in his career and now two together.'

'He must be near death if he's taken two days off. I remember he only took a half-day when his parents fell down that disused mineshaft near St Ives, and then he worked extra hours to make up the time.'

Henry nods as he listens, the curse established once more in his mind as an absolute truth.

He stops outside the training room. After a moment's pause – should I or shouldn't I? – he goes in, emerging thirty seconds later, trying not to laugh.

He reaches the secretary's room and leans in, hanging on the lintel.

'Is he in?'

'Yes, dear. Do you want me to—'

'No. I'll just pop in.'

Henry goes in without knocking.

The Bitch is seated, both hands on his lap, leaning over a case file, the pince-nez he affects perched on the bridge of his nose.

'Bob,' says Henry, marching in.

'You,' says the Bitch.

'You were expecting me?'

'I was intending to summon you.'

'Oh, yes?' says Henry, taking a seat. 'Why would that be?'

The Bitch opens his mouth, but Henry interrupts.

'No, don't tell me. Mr Thorough. Ed. He's been talking. That guy . . .'

'Mr Brinks,' says the Bitch, closing the file, taking off his ridiculous eyeglasses. 'This is not a time for brevity.'

'Levity. You mean levity.'

The Bitch flinches. 'I would—'

Henry butts in again. 'No. You're right. Brevity, levity, whatever. It's not the moment.'

'I spoke with Immigration Officer Thorough yesterday.'

'You showed him the letter, right?'

The Bitch stops, thinks. 'What letter?' he asks archly.

'Come on, Bob. The letter. You did get it?'

'You admit to writing it?'

'I admit to nothing.'

'Ed Thorough knew it was you who sent it. He told me that he had confronted you with your continuing infraction of the immigration rules. I am persuaded that the letter was an elaborate smokescreen, an attempt to disguise the true guilt in this matter.'

'Ed told you that?'

'It's my own reading of the situation.'

Henry sighs, shakes his head. 'It looks bad for me, then?'

'These are grave matters. Criminal matters.'

Henry bites his lip. 'So what now? Down to the office, a rummage in the old locker?'

'Duty requires me to authorise a search.'

'You know, of course, that it's a setup?'

'If there is evidence against you . . .'

'Oh, it'll be there. Immigration Officer Thorough will have made sure of that.'

The Bitch takes his turn to sigh. 'If you insist on making unfounded allegations against respected members of staff, you'll find yourself even more isolated.'

'Wouldn't want that.'

'I see no further reason for delay. Would you wish for a representative of your union to be present during the search of your locker?'

Henry shrugs. 'No need.'

'Very well. You'll come with me.'

Henry leans out of his chair and rummages in his knapsack. 'No,' he says. 'There's no need because you're not going to search my locker. In fact, you're going to get Thorough to come down here and you're going to tell him to take out whatever he's put in there.'

Now the Bitch is angry, stamping his foot, eyes screwing up, fat little fists clenched tight. He shouts now. 'You little shit! What do you think gives you the—'

Henry waves a videotape next to his ear, which rattles gently.

'What? What is this?'

'You'd better sit down,' says Henry, getting up.

He goes to the corner of the Bitch's office and brings the video camera and TV into a more central position. With a wire taken from his bag, he connects the camera to the telly and puts the cassette into it.

'I've edited it down to the good bits,' he explains, switching on the TV.

The static on-screen fuzzes gently and then quickly settles itself into the view of the Bitch at his desk.

'You . . . You did this?' asks the Bitch.

'I admit to nothing,' says Henry.

After it's over, six minutes later, Henry rises again and takes out the video. 'I know it's pedantic,' he says, 'but just in case you'd thought about it, I've made several copies and they're in various . . .' he pauses. 'You know what I mean.'

The Bitch nods, ghastly white.

'This is despicable,' he mutters.

'Worse than deliberately framing your colleagues?'

'I would never . . . I don't condone . . . What is it that you want?'

Henry's smile sharpens. 'What is it that I want? What is it that I want *from life?*'

The Bitch recognises the echo of his own words.

'What I want from life is something you can't give me, Bob. What I want is to erase the last five shitty years since I crossed the threshold into this zoo. I want my innocence back, Bob. That's what I really want from life. I want my soul back.'

The Bitch snorts his scorn.

'There's no need to be like that. After all, I'm making this easy for you. All you have to do is call Thorough off. Any sniff of me being set up and the video goes to Miriam Cooper, among others.'

'Blackmail?'

'No other word for it,' Henry smiles.

The Bitch takes a hard breath through the nose.

'That's all you want? For me to speak to Thorough?'

Henry sits down again, wrapping the video cable into a ball around his fist. He purses his lips together before speaking. 'Not quite all.'

'Well?' The Bitch is impatient. 'What else?'

Henry scratches his ear. 'Sandgate.'

The Bitch snorts. 'Impossible. Absurd.'

'Why absurd? There's a vacancy. Everybody knows that.'

'It's been taken. Richard Foster's transfer has been approved.'

'You're going to let him go after what happened with Jimmy Craddock yesterday?'

The Bitch shakes his head, exasperated. 'I have no . . . It was Foster who had his nose bitten off. I hardly think . . .'

'Oh, yes. I know that,' says Henry with a shake of the head. 'But you know, I was there. It was Dick who started it. Anyone will tell you.'

The Bitch pouts. 'Is that the case?'

'Just ask anybody. Just ask Ed.'

Henry's on his way out when he bumps into Ronan, who's laughing, excited.

'Awright, man,' he says. 'What are you doing with them clothes on?'

Henry opens his mouth but doesn't get the chance to form a word.

'Never mind, never mind. There's something here you've got to see. You just have to see it.'

'What?'

'Come on.' He beckons him out of the door and towards the control.

'You know Rex Gibbons retired?'

'Oh, yeah. He said he was taking up some consultancy job with . . . Royal Sheikh, wasn't it?'

Ronan stops, mouth open. 'Is that what he said?'

'Erm, something like that . . . "A variety of work" – that was it.'

Ronan laughs out loud. 'You have just got to fucking see *this.*'

And there, at the far end of the control, stands Rex Gibbons, who only hours before was putting the finishing touches to Henry's annual report and today is wearing a silly green cap and pushing an old woman in a veil around in her wheelchair. He's trying to look cheerful to the small group of IOs that have gathered around him – Speerpoint takes off his hat to try on for himself and one or two of the others are patting him on the pate – but he's snorting even more than usual and the look behind his eyes is that of a crushed soul.

' "A variety of work," ' repeats Ronan, laughing still. 'They've got him pushing raspberry ripples around the terminal. My cup runneth over.'

Henry looks on. In the black quarter of his heart, there's some pleasure in seeing Gibbons humiliated in this way. He understands why the others are taking their chance to wreak a ruthless revenge on him for his years of spitefulness to them. But in the end, the scene is pure Terminal C: one of raw, almost unbearable cruelty.

He's not laughing. Just glad to be out of it. That's all.

Two Months Later

Henry sits by the window, legs on the desk. Between his feet, the second ferry of the day makes her way out of the harbour. By the time she returns, Henry's shift will be long over.

A horn sounds, sending a flock of seagulls scuttling before they recongregate in much the same position as before.

Henry yawns and stretches. The piece of paper on his lap falls off and floats to the ground. He doesn't make any attempt to pick it up.

A couple of months in Sandgate and he feels like a different person, calmer, at ease. And the money – he's almost doubled his salary, what with travelling expenses and the incidental overtime. Not forgetting the Crown Transfer he was given, all his moving expenses paid, all that nasty negative equity swallowed up in one go. He likes his new house. Nice view of the sea.

Since his arrival, he hasn't had a single case. Not one. There's no computer at Sandgate, just a blackboard where all the live cases are numbered. At the moment there are seven, three of which have been ongoing for a couple of years.

Henry's got a girlfriend now. She's Rhianon, a physiotherapist who works in the sports club Henry's joined. They slept together for the first time last night. He's thinking about her quite a lot.

He's even bought himself a camera and started trying to put a short film together. About a bloke who . . . well, he's still working on it . . .

One other person in the office. His name is Kevin. Big bloke, moustache. There is something on Kevin's mind. His brow creases before he speaks. 'Just run it by me one more time.'

'Which part?'

'The reason. The compassionate.'

Henry yawns. 'The doctor said I was hypersensitive to the frequencies being given off by the terminal building.'

'You mean like cockpit radios?'

'No. The building is giving off these vibrations. The building itself, yeah? It's the metal ores in the superstructure,' says Henry, rolling his eyes out of Kevin's view.

'Fuck me. And these give off frequencies?'

'Yup.'

'And you can hear them?'

'Not really. They're too high-pitched.'

'So, like dogs can hear them?'

'Well, no,' says Henry, tiring of the subject. 'There aren't packs of beagles running around, biting people and chasing jumbo jets down the runway. These frequencies are like waves, rays. Negative rays. It's called sick building syndrome. Being there made me sick. Literally.'

'What symptoms did you have, then?'

'Headaches, fatigue, stress. All chronic.' Henry drops his legs off the table and spins round in his chair, facing Kevin. 'The voices told me I had to get a transfer.'

'What voices?'

'The voices in my head. That's what the frequencies were doing. They put the voices in my head and then the voices started talking to me until the point came when I was just a vehicle through which they could speak. Refuse, they were saying, refuse, refuse them all and I was powerless to stop them.'

Kevin scrunches up a piece of paper into a ball and throws it at Henry.

'Shut up, you daft sod.'

Henry laughs.

'The talk was,' Kevin says, 'that we were supposed to be getting Dick Foster down here. Nobody was looking forward to that.'

'Yeah, well, you know. I think he was in the frame. Until the fight.'

'This is the fight with Jimmy Craddock?'

'You know Jimmy?'

'We used to be at Dover together, before he got a disciplinary for shagging this girl from Sierra Leone in the detainees' toilet. Good laugh, Jimmy. I heard he bit Foster's ear off.'

'Something like that. Foster got kicked to Terminal A on a disciplinary for gross provocation.'

'Yeah. Not like Jimmy to do something like that to another IO. Not without good reason.'

'Not like Jimmy,' Henry concurs.

'I heard that the Bitch come down on Foster like a sack of shit, insisted that he lost the transfer here.'

'Suppose so.'

'Which left you next on the list.'

'Lucky me,' Henry says.

He spins back to the window and puts his feet up again.

A memory makes him smile. A Terminal C memory, a memory of his last day, when he stood at the training room door, pausing a moment before going in.

Once inside, he slipped off his knapsack and took out one of the two copies of the video he'd brought with him. He went to the bank of training films that nobody ever watches, picked a copy of *Get in on the (Immigration) Act (1971)!* and swapped the tape inside the box for one of his.

One day somebody would, for a reason too obscure to imagine, decide to have a look at that tape.

The tape is of the Bitch, in his office.

There is a knock at the door.

The Bitch rises from his chair in anticipation and takes off his jacket, hanging it over the back of the chair.

'Come,' he says.

Sharon Barber enters the room. 'Bob,' she says quietly, a little coldly.

'Sharon,' he replies. 'I wanted to see you.'

'Yes?'

'I thought it was about time we discussed your report again. Your prospects for promotion.'

Sharon nods. 'I thought it would be that,' she says, moving nearer him.

The Bitch slips the braces off his shoulders, allowing his trousers to drop to his ankles. Turning to face his desk, he bends forward slightly and pulls down his black Y-fronts. He then plants both hands on the desk.

'You want me to . . .?'

'That's correct. You'll find it in my briefcase.'

Sharon clicks the case open.

'In the plastic bag,' he says.

She pulls out a blue plastic bag and turns it upside down.

A thin, green dildo clatters on to the desk.

With a grimace, she picks it up, allowing it to dangle between thumb and forefinger and moves behind the Bitch. She stoops, awkwardly, dildo in hand and gently probes the Bitch's rump with its blunt end.

'You'll have to squat a little more. I need to . . .'

'Very well. Are you . . .?'

'If you just . . .'

'How . . .?'

'I think a bit further . . . Just, yes . . . I don't want to injure you . . .'

'OK. Just . . . there.'

The Bitch emits a hissing moan. Sharon stands upright and pushes the plastic dick up his arse with the flat of her hand. As she lets go, the Bitch gingerly turns to face her. He sports an erection, fat and pink, as if Sharon somehow has pushed the synthetic phallus too far.

'Ready?' she asks him, matter-of-factly.

'Proceed,' he replies through clenched teeth.

Leaning back, half-sitting on the desk, he reaches with his

left hand for a small audio tape recorder. He pushes a button with his thumb and brings it to his mouth.

'Memo,' he says, his voice a trifle higher-pitched than usual. 'Promotion report for Mrs Sharon Barber, Chief Immigration Officer.'

Mrs Sharon Barber, CIO, drops to her knees. She cups the Bitch's balls in her hand and begins to fellate him as he talks.

'Mrs Barber's performance over the past year has been exemplary,' he grunts. 'She has shown exceptional development and operates at a level well . . . ssssss . . . beyond the requirements of her post . . .'

Sharon's head starts to bob harder, back and forth on the Bitch's cock.

' . . . her man management has steadily improved over the reporting year and she is well capable of bringing out the best in both her colleagues and those suborrrrrrrdinate to her . . .'

Sharon begins to squeeze the Bitch's bollocks, increasing the length and speed of her lolly strokes, expertly flicking back his flap of foreskin with the tips of her teeth. The Bitch's register rises.

' . . . In supervising the refusal, detention and removal of problem immigration cases, Mrs Barber has proven herself to be an enormous asset to the de-part-ment . . . *haaaaaarrr* . . . and is the very personification of the firm but fair controoooooooo . . .'

The Bitch's climax imminent, Sharon gently applies upward pressure on the root of the dildo, sending the Port Commissioner into orbit.

'FIRM BUT FAIR! FIRM BUT FAIR! FIRM BUT FAIR!' he screams into the Dictaphone as he drains his testicles over Sharon's tonsils.

She rises to her feet. The Bitch falls back on to the desk, sobbing.

She stands and waits. The Bitch puts out a hand asking her

to wait as he catches his breath. Slowly, he brings the recorder back to his mouth.

'In conclusion, I support Mrs Barber's promotion in the strongest possible terms.'

Sharon smiles and puts out a hand. The Bitch ejects the cassette and drops it into her palm.

'I'll put this straight up to the typist,' she says, closing the door behind her.

And if ever, thinks Henry, anyone does decide to sit through that copy of *Get in on the (Immigration) Act (1971)!* , his or her entertainment would be rounded off by a full length view of Bob Gascoigne slowly retracting an eight-inch rubber cock from his own anal canal.

He laughs involuntarily at the thought, catching it too late, so it comes out as a snort from the back of his throat.

'What?' says Kevin.

'Nothing,' says Henry, rubbing the bridge of his nose, trying to hide his giggles.

'What?' insists Kevin.

'Nothing, nothing,' Henry tells him, leaning down to pick up the letter which has dropped from his lap. 'Have you seen this?'

'What is it?'

'It's a denunce.' Denunciatory letter, this means.

'Excellent,' says Kevin. 'What's it say?'

Henry reads it out loud. It says:

> Dear Sirmadam
>
> I'm written to tel that there is restorant in sandgate where all waiters do not have Hom Office papers (immigraton). It is the India restaurant on ravenstone st., calling tigger of Punjab. all waiters not have visas, all jump off lory at roundbout where A274 + A17

enjoy congress together. please also not from punjab, they are all bengali boys.

friend of taxpayer and believer in english(British) ways

Henry hands it over. Kevin has a look.

'I know who wrote this.'

'You do?'

'Oh, yeah. It's that feller that runs the other curry house, the one down by the marina. I recognise his handwriting. We've got a bloody drawer full of these. Puts on the crap English, mind. Went to Dulwich College or somewhere. He's been trying to put Rashid out of business for years.'

He flicks the paper over, looks at the back, then reads it again.

'Still,' he says, 'I suppose we have to act on it.'

'Do we?'

'We ought to. Chiefy'll think we're slacking.'

Kevin picks up the phone on his desk and calls a number from his Rolodex.

'Hello, is that Rashid?. Hello, mate. It's Kevin from the immigration office . . . yeah, listen, Rashid, we're going to have to pop down for a visit . . . yeah, official, that's right . . . no, not straight away, let's say about . . . well, look, what's good for you? . . . about forty minutes . . . all right, call it an hour . . . yes, Rashid, we will have to look in the kitchens . . . yeah, well obviously, anyone who's not legal we'll have to pull in, won't we? . . . Of course, if they're not there, we're not going to pick them up, are we? (Rolls his eyes at Henry.) . . . I know you're running a business, Rashid . . . Jesus, just tell them to come back in an hour and a half. We'll be gone by then . . . What's that? . . . Yeah, yeah . . . I'll just check with my colleague . . .'

He cups the receiver in his hand. 'He's asking if you want something to eat?'

Henry shakes his head. 'I'm skint.'

Kevin laughs, shakes his head at Henry's naivety.

'Yeah,' he says down the line to Rashid. 'Two specials . . . a few poppadoms. Why not? Well, we're going to need *something* to wash it down with . . . Yeah, yeah. See you soon.'

Kevin puts the phone down.

'Christ,' he comments, glancing at his watch. 'Yeah, that should give them enough time to scarper. We'll give them an hour. That's the thing about this job,' he adds, picking up the local newspaper, shaking it loose. 'People just haven't got a clue about how we operate. Not a clue.'